Her B
Cowboy's Fake Marriage

A billionaire cowboy in need of a wife, a waitress in need of a miracle and the offer she can't refuse.

The last thing cowboy Wade McCoy expects when his beloved billionaire granddaddy dies is for him to require Wade to marry in order to save the vast McCoy Ranch that they both loved and built together. But that is exactly his granddaddy's requirement: Wade has to marry within three months, *stay* married for at least three months or he loses it all, for him and his brothers.

He doesn't like it, but his granddaddy didn't raise him to walk away from anything and there has never been a challenge he couldn't win...with no plans to lose the ranch he loves now Wade just has to find a woman who will go along with this crazy idea.

Allie Jordon is desperate. Every bad piece of luck that could have befallen her has done so and now, after losing everything, including her sweet father, she needs funds to get her injured mother the best care available or she just might lose her too.

A chance meeting with a lonely looking cowboy at the truck stop she's waitressing at could change her life...if she says yes to an absolutely off-the-wall proposal he's offering her it could be the miracle she's been praying for.

You're going to love this new series about two billionaire brothers determined to marry off their grandsons...one's doing it from the grave using his last will and testament.

HER BILLIONAIRE COWBOY'S FAKE MARRIAGE

McCoy Billionaire Brothers, Book One

HOPE MOORE

Her Billionaire Cowboy's Fake Marriage
Copyright © 2019 Hope Moore

CHAPTER ONE

"*You have got to be kidding me.*"

Wade McCoy stared at his granddaddy's lawyer, Mr. Cal Emerson.

The thin-faced, somber-eyed man's scowl did not look as if he were kidding. Though his intense eyes were full of sorrow and solemnity today. He had, after all, been one of J.D. McCoy's best friends. Wade and his brothers had lost a grandfather but Mr. Emerson had lost a buddy.

And then there was the significance of what he'd just told Wade, Todd, and Morgan. That would also play into the graveness of the moment and expression.

Wade had a feeling his expression mirrored Mr. Emerson's.

Morgan looked more perplexed than angry. Todd wore a tightly controlled expression.

They'd just come from the graveside and were sitting in their granddaddy's office, surrounded by the scents of leather furniture, a lot of dark wood, and thick Western art rugs that J.D. McCoy had loved. His essence surrounded them. That, and the force of nature that he'd been, still lingered.

"This is ridiculous." Morgan crossed his arms from where he stood, next to the massive fireplace.

"It doesn't sound like him," Todd added, leaning forward in his chair, his elbows on his knees. "Why would he do that to us, but most especially to Wade? That's a lot of pressure on him."

"Tell me about it." Wade leveled a penetrating gaze on Mr. Emerson. "Just to be completely clear. You said my granddaddy left me and my brothers the ranch, but *only* if I find a *wife* before the end of three months? And then stay married for at least three months."

The lawyer placed his hands flat on the desk on either side of Wade's granddaddy's will that lay open in front of him. "Yes, that is what I said. And Wade, he was very clear that those were his requirements in order for you to keep McCoy Enterprises Ranch and Cattle Division and that includes the oil rights. He thought maybe you needed a little nudge. He knew how much you loved this place. And he knew how negative you were about marriage. He hated that in the worst way. He told me that the ranch was too big to have you wandering around all by your lonesome. He said you needed to build a family out there and enjoy it. Those were his words. But to be clear, your shares in the hotel chain and other investments are not in jeopardy."

And there it was, the announcement that had disbelief strangling him with angry claws that tightened around Wade's throat. He hung his head and rubbed his forehead as a drumbeat intensified behind his eyes. His heart ached at the loss of the man he'd loved with every ounce of his being. The man he'd respected beyond anyone ever. *Why had Granddaddy done this?* His mind clicked through everything that had happened in the months before he died. *What had happened to cause this?* Nothing that he could think of.

"It doesn't make sense. Cal, this just does not make sense." Morgan glared, looking as if he, too, were getting a headache. He focused on Wade. "Did he take a fall and hit his head or something?"

Wade shook his head. "No fall that I know of." He'd been wondering whether he'd fallen off his horse and hit his head, gone crazy, or lost his faculties but Wade was coming up empty.

"Had he shown any signs of senility?" Todd crossed his arms. His brows were nearly touching. "He seemed fine the last time he came over to see me."

Wade racked his brain. *Had he missed the signs?* He replayed the months, but there didn't seem to be anything about his attitude or his actions that would have led Wade to believe he was anything but the astute businessman that he'd always been. They had just gone on a three-day cattle roundup and his granddaddy, though he was seventy-seven years old, had ridden straighter in the saddle than any of the cowboys who worked for him. He'd slept in a bedroll under the stars like the rest of them, enjoying the feeling of doing it the way his ancestors had done it years ago.

"No," he growled, feeling helpless to figure it out. "There was nothing wrong with his brain at the time of his death or any time before that. Did he recently amend this will?"

Cal Emerson nodded. "He did, but he was every bit of sound mind when he did it."

Todd stood and moved to the window then back to the chair. He was finding nothing humorous about any of this, the hard angles of his face grim. "Why?"

Wade knew his brother was as frustrated as he was. "Todd, he was his same ole bossy and demanding self. On the roundup, he told the men exactly what to do, when to do it, and how to do it. Nothing wrong with his thinking."

A melancholy smile momentarily settled on Todd's face. "He was good at giving directions."

"Too good at it," Morgan grunted. "And still doing it from the grave. He always did want to control us."

"I don't call it that." Wade refused to agree with Morgan after years of disagreeing over their granddaddy. "He just had a strong will. And so do you."

"Whatever." Morgan's expression remained dark.

Wade ground his teeth, holding back anything that would make the situation worse. He knew his granddaddy hadn't lost his mind. Meaning, therefore, that there was no easy reasoning for this craziness. Why in the world had he put in his will that Wade had to get married before the end of three months? Get married or lose *everything*.

Todd sighed. "I don't get Granddaddy going to this extreme just to get Wade's attention. And what about me and Morgan? We weren't as close to him as Wade, so there must be something really crazy in there in store for us. He's probably going to give me an ultimatum on the vineyard. I'm sure we won't get off free and clear, right?"

"This is all I'm able to reveal at the moment. Your granddaddy left a complicated will for McCoy Enterprises, which includes the McCoy Ranch and Cattle Division, the McCoy Stonewall Jelly and Wine Division and McCoy Enterprises Hotel and Resort Division. In due time all will be revealed."

All their gazes collided. Wade cleared his throat, his mind churning. Wade yanked his hat from his head and worried it between his fingers. *He had to get married.* The news gnawed at him like a hungry coyote.

If he had to get married in three months to save his ranch, he'd do it.

"I know Granddaddy didn't lose his mind, and I haven't either. Whatever it takes to keep the Rocking M in my family, I'll do." Especially considering, for some reason, the task was on his shoulders to keep it in the family for all of his brothers. If he didn't get married, Todd and Morgan lost out on the ranch too.

Morgan was right on the point that Granddaddy liked to give orders. But he hadn't been able to tell the good Lord when it was his time to go. His death had been sudden and unexpected.

Nope, the Lord had decided a week ago, while J.D. McCoy was eating pecan pie at Dixie's Diner, that J.D.'s time was up. And in a blink of an eye, he was gone. Wade had been sitting across the booth from his granddaddy when the heart attack had taken him.

No warning, no second chance at a miracle. He'd just been gone.

There hadn't been a ride in an ambulance and a doctor going in and doing surgery to repair heart valves…no, it had been massive. One and done.

A knockout punch in the quickest form.

Why did some people get a shot at a miracle and others didn't? Anger balled up inside Wade. He took a deep breath and yanked his gaze from where he'd been staring out the window. "My gut tells me this is a bluff."

Wade watched Cal's eyes and every facial expression for a sign that the lawyer might give him that said Wade had hit upon the truth. Because if anyone knew what J.D. was up to, it would be his buddy Cal. But Cal wasn't one of the best lawyers in

Texas and the country for nothing. He had a poker face that was legendary. And it was firmly in place. If he knew more than what he was telling him, his expression didn't give it away.

J.D. McCoy had been ambitious and a hard worker. Yeah, ranching was always more profitable when there was oil on the place, but Granddaddy had built a respected chain of hotels and resorts too, and many other investments, including the extremely successful jelly and wine from the vineyard. And then there was the oil, which had complicated things sometimes. It had sure complicated Wade's life...he'd never been able to hide from it.

"This is it, boys. The way he wanted it."

Wade hung his head and tried to let the frustrations go. One thing his granddaddy had always taught him was if you had a job to do, you got it done and you didn't bellyache about it. You didn't procrastinate; you just manned up and got it done.

And then there was the family responsibility. That took precedence over everything.

"So, what'll it be, son?"

Wade heard Granddaddy's question as if he were standing in the middle of the office, his Stetson cocked back, with that crooked grin and challenge in his steel-blue eyes.

Wade lifted his head, and he met Mr. Emerson's eyes with his stare. "Three months of marriage and then the ranch is ours? If not, then Morgan and Todd lose their shares too?" *Did he think if he kept questioning it that the answer would be different?*

Mr. Emerson nodded. "Yes. You're the first domino, and if you fall, they all fall. But that doesn't mean they don't have their own stipulations on you all inheriting other portions of the will."

Wade groaned. *Granddaddy, what have you done?* "So, when do Morgan and Todd find out what their stipulations are?"

Mr. Emerson leaned back in his chair. "Can I speak frankly?"

"Of course," Morgan said, his voice tight with restraint.

"You know we don't want you to speak any other way. We are clueless here, and quite frankly, at a loss.

I want to speak frankly, too…you're his lawyer. Why didn't you advise him against these shenanigans?"

"Exactly," Morgan snapped.

"I have to agree." Todd hitched a brow.

Mr. Emerson quirked his lips. "Now you McCoy boys are sounding like J.D.," he drawled, his Texas accent coming out. "You three boys and I all know that when your granddaddy got a burr up his butt or under his saddle, nobody was talking him out of it."

"True," Wade said. "Go on."

"J.D. has been worried for a while now that the ranch out there was going to dry up, with no heirs. You're the only one living on it who is his own flesh and blood. He built that ranch for y'all to take it over. It was his legacy to you three, and y'all were letting him down. He was desperate. Morgan and him haven't gotten along in a long time. He and Todd butted heads some too—both were stubborn and a lot alike. Todd was never attached to the ranch like you, but he's attached to the grapes and the land at the McCoy Stonewall Jelly and Wine Division. He was always scared he was going to die and there wasn't going to be any great-grandkids to carry on what he'd started. Wade, you are not the marrying kind. You have never shown any inkling or any inclination toward marriage after—"

"True." Morgan agreed.

"I work all the time. Just like he did. It's my business if I don't want to get married."

"I know that," Morgan snapped, frustration in his voice too. "What Delta did—"

Wade held his hand up and halted his words. "I don't care to get into that. Not now, not ever." He didn't like being forced into anything. "So, when are the terms of the rest of the will going to be known for Morgan and Todd?"

"Only after you fulfill your part."

"Did Granddaddy give you any hints or did he have any ideas about how I'm supposed to make this happen?"

Mr. Emerson chuckled, took his glasses off, and laid them on the desk as he rubbed his eyes. "Wade, you're a smart fella. He figured you'd figure something out. I think he's probably going to enjoy the show, because I'm like your granddaddy. I have a feeling you're going to figure out how to come out of this on top. But, I have to warn you, when you walk out that door, the clock starts ticking."

Morgan looked grim. "As much as I hope we don't lose the ranch, you don't have to do this, Wade."

"I agree with Morgan." Todd's eyes narrowed dangerously. "Granddaddy has gone too far. I can tell you I'm not marrying if he throws something like this at me. I'll walk away. I just don't get it. When he called me when I was recovering at the hospital, he never mentioned anything like this. It's just not right."

Wade took in their words, but this was his decision to make and only his.

He stood and slowly placed his hat back on his head. He didn't know how he was going to do it, but he had to figure out something, because if there was one thing that was for certain, it was he would not lose this ranch. "Fellas, as crazy as it sounds, Granddaddy figured I could do this. He's challenged me. Just like he challenged me every day all the days of my life. And he's right in his thinking. I'm going to do it

13

because too much of what I've worked for is riding on this. And there is no way on God's green earth that I'm going to let him down. Or us. If he thought I could do this, then I will. Mark my words, Mr. Emerson, by the end of ninety days, I will be married."

Allie Jordan was tired. Her head hurt, her back hurt, her feet hurt. But that was nothing on how much her heart hurt. She pushed that pain away, knowing that dwelling on it wouldn't help ease something that couldn't be undone. But work could help. Work and a paycheck was the only thing that could help her now.

That and a miracle.

She worked a double shift at the busy truck stop outside of Tyler, Texas. Her life was a mess, and the job was a lifesaver in a time when she didn't have time to figure anything else out, and she needed the flexibility of the hours she could get. And those were in never-ending supply because there an almost never-ending flow of hungry truckers stopping in. It made it hard for two waitresses and really hard on one when, like tonight, one had called in sick.

She'd walked miles from table to order window and back to tables, delivering food. Becky, the other waitress, had called in sick and had hated it, Allie was sure. But a stomach bug was going around, and Allie was just thankful she hadn't gotten it. She couldn't afford to be sick.

Picking up a platter of pancakes and bacon from the order window, she gave Pete, the cook, a weary smile. "Thanks." Then she headed off to deliver the feast to the cowboy sitting in the corner, nursing his coffee that she'd refilled numerous times.

He looked about as worried as she was tired. She had noticed him when he first came in. He was tall, broad-shouldered, and had that cowboy swagger that she tried hard to ignore. Cowboys gave her indigestion. And considering she lived in Texas, born and raised in Texas, and was raised around cowboys, she had indigestion all the time. But really, she only got it when they smiled at her, or paid attention to her, or tried to get her to go out with them…she now had a cowboy rule.

She had learned a long time ago, up close and personal, that the cowboy myth that they were honorable was, in fact, a lie. She had had her fill of cowboys and their lies. But this guy, when he walked in—*be still her heart*—there was no denying that one look at him and she had forgotten the golden rule she lived by, and that was to avoid cowboys at all costs.

He'd looked tired and preoccupied, and yet, he'd still given her a soft thank-you when she'd set water and a mug in front of him and asked whether he'd like coffee.

"Yes, thank you," he'd drawled, then rubbed his temple and stared out the window as she'd filled his cup. Something about him had her curiosity up, even when she knew better. Even when she had no time to even daydream about a handsome man—cowboy or not, it didn't matter. She had no time for a man in her life right now, and no heart for it anyway. *So why then was this cowboy setting butterflies swirling in her chest?*

He didn't smile, but he was gorgeous, a little sad-looking or worried—she thought he looked more sad than worried, and she knew how that felt. She was both herself. Maybe it was a combination of both for him, too. Whatever it was, he was pretty occupied with his thoughts and she felt a pull toward him. Which, for her, had spelled disaster not but a couple of months ago; she'd lost her savings and her dream all because she'd tried to be kind to someone. And then she'd lost more. Her heart clutched; she pushed the grief away and focused on her work. *Thank goodness for work.*

The man had been drinking and thinking and she'd finally asked him again whether he needed anything to eat. He'd hardly looked at her, he was so deep in thought.

"Pancakes are great," she'd finally offered on his third refill. "Bacon is thick and Pete is a master at frying it. I'll order you some, okay?"

The man didn't look hungry, so why she was pushing food on him, she wasn't certain. No, it was easy to see that the man wasn't starving. He filled out his starched shirt and starched jeans too well to be starving. He had thick, firm muscles, broad shoulders, and a narrow waist to go with strong, long, jean-clad legs. He looked about as healthy as a man could be—not that she was noticing.

Or had the heart for it, she reminded herself now as she approached with the pancakes.

He smiled a distracted smile as she set them down in front of him. *Maybe he, too, had lost someone he loved.* The thought had her heart clenching and aching, not wishing that on anyone.

"Here you go. I promise you, you're going to like them. They may even put a smile on your face. A genuine smile. I'll get you more coffee."

"Thanks." He focused on her as if looking at her for the first time. "What's your name?"

She had forgotten to wear her name tag today. "Allie. What's yours?" *Why did she ask him that?* She didn't ask people their information if she could sidestep it. She didn't get friendly with the customers here. No, they hit on her too much and she wasn't having any of that. She came to work alone and she left alone.

"The name is Wade…Wade McCoy. Nice to meet you, Allie. I'm sorry if I was rude or seemed to be brushing you off. I didn't mean it. These pancakes smell delicious, and so does the bacon. Just like you said."

"Oh no, you weren't. Wait till you taste them." He was polite, even distracted as he was. She smiled and went to get the coffee. She glanced over her shoulder. Something just wasn't right about the guy. She watched him rub his temple, and then he picked up his fork and knife, cut into the pancakes, and took a bite. He set his fork and knife down and stared out the window again.

She carried the carafe back across the diner. It was fairly quiet in the diner now. The few who were there had their food and drinks and were busy eating. Maybe that's why she was preoccupied with him—because she finally had a moment to breathe.

He was still staring out the window when she poured his coffee, the pancakes forgotten.

"Is everything all right?" she asked, concern overriding her good sense. "I can't help but notice that you just look like something's wrong."

He pushed the plate away from him and watched

19

as she filled the coffee mug again.

"Have you ever felt like you were failing everybody who was counting on you?"

His words were heavy and struck her heart like direct hits. He looked up at her as he asked the question, and she was caught by the deep blue of his eyes. They seemed to drill into her, and they were right on target with what she felt deep inside her heart.

"Every day of my life," she said. "It's not a good way to feel. Is that what's wrong with you?"

His brow creased and his jaw clenched. "You feel that way? I'm sorry if you do. It's most definitely not a good way to feel."

She swallowed hard. The lump formed in her throat, and the knot caused her heart to ache. "No, it's not, and I'm real sorry you feel that way. I wouldn't wish it on my worst enemy, to tell you the truth. But you just don't look like somebody who would fail people. I mean, me…I totally get it, but you look very capable."

"I could say the same thing about you. I don't know what makes you feel like you're failing people around you, but I am on the verge of losing everything that ever meant anything to my granddaddy and despite my best intentions, I haven't done what I need to do to prevent it from happening."

"Well, that's just terrible. I mean, you can't do anything about it?"

"Well, I could have, but it's pretty much too late. I had three months, but the deadline runs out in three days and what I need to do was impossible to do in three months. I was determined to do it but I couldn't go through with it. Now, three days? No way. For the first time in my life, I feel like I'm defeated, and I don't like it."

She felt for him. Whatever it was that was bothering him was eating him up. Feeling like you were failing those you loved didn't sit right with her either. They had that in common. She didn't feel as if she were talking to a stranger, but she felt as if she were talking to a friend. "I wish there was something I could do to help you."

He gave a bittersweet laugh. "Allie, there is nothing you can do. Unless, of course, you wanted to marry a total stranger for a big paycheck. Because that's what I need. I need a temporary wife, and I need her before the end of three days."

Stunned, she stared at him, unsure she'd just heard him correctly. She couldn't believe what she was hearing. She had heard of things like this, seen it in a lot of romance movies and romance books, but had she ever met anyone who really needed to get married like that? Marry a total stranger? No, she never had.

She swallowed hard and tried to still her rapidly pounding heart. "W-why do you have to get married in three days, and what do you lose if you don't?"

He heaved a resigned sigh. "My granddaddy stipulated it in his will, and he had his reasons, though I have to say I question them. But he gave me three months after he died to get married, or else I lose everything—I lose the ranch, I lose the legacy, I lose it all. All that I've helped him build with my own sweat and hard work. And love. And the bad thing is, my brothers' inheritance relies on me getting married and fulfilling my end of the bargain. So, it all rests on my shoulders. And it's not going to happen. I've failed."

He took a drink of his coffee, closed his eyes and rubbed the bridge of his nose.

She studied him. Her heart beat a triple-time rhythm now, and her palms were hot and clammy. She swallowed hard. *Could this really be happening?* "Wade." She set the coffee carafe down as she slid into the seat across the table from him.

He opened his eyes and his brows creased as he saw her sitting across from him. "What's wrong?"

"Wade, what…what does the woman who marries you get out of the bargain if you were to find someone who would marry you in three days so you could save your legacy and help you make your grandpa proud?" *Hadn't he said something about a big paycheck?*

He sat up straight now. His eyes narrowed and his jaw hardened. "Well, Granddaddy left her a little something. Actually, a big something, with several zeroes behind it. Why? Why are you asking me that?" He sounded oddly both wary and hopeful.

Allie's heart thundered. She took a deep breath and ran her damp palms over the skirt of her uniform as she stared at him. "Because, well, my mama, she's...she's in the hospital. And needs to be transferred to a rehab center right now. But they need a payment and I don't have it yet." She fought off the lump in her chest. "Two months ago, my mom and my dad were in a terrible car wreck, and my dad...we lost him. My mama was hurt really bad and she needs constant care in a facility right now. She is in a coma, and they don't know when or if she'll come out of it. Insurance won't pay for all of her needs and I don't have the money for the best care for her. I'm working every extra shift I can but I'm at my wit's end on what I'll do. She'll go to a facility but not the one she needs the most. So, I was just wondering what exactly I would get if I agreed to marry you and help you save your legacy?"

Wade stared at her with sympathy. "I'm sorry about your dad. That's not long after I lost my granddaddy. Grief is ridiculous. It's just awful, and I'm so sorry. I'm real sorry about your mama, too. I can tell you that if you agree to marry me within three days, and then stay married to me for at least three months, I'll make sure your mama gets what she needs, even if my granddaddy's legacy isn't enough to pay for what she's going through, because I'm pretty sure that your bills are high."

She couldn't believe she had asked him that. She couldn't believe she was about to do this. But she was, because this serious-eyed, handsome cowboy was the answer to her prayers.

She took a deep breath and met his eyes with a steady gaze that took all her willpower to maintain. "Then, if that's the case, Wade McCoy, you've got yourself a bride—or should I say a wife—if you want one. If I'll do?"

His expression slackened, his nice mouth parted slightly, and his brow, already creased, deepened. Then, as if seeing the certainty in her eyes, he nodded and held out his hand. "You'll certainly do," he drawled, even slower than before as those amazing eyes held hers.

Was this real? Was she being conned?

A shiver raced through her and she almost told him she'd made a mistake. Couldn't go through with it.

But the words didn't come. Instead, she hoped with all her heart it worked, hoped it was real because this was the best option that she had.

It was the only option she had.

CHAPTER TWO

Wade couldn't believe this was happening. She was a waitress at a truck stop outside of Tyler, and she was offering to marry him.

The day he had learned about the stipulations in his granddaddy's will, he had been determined that he wouldn't let the family down. He had three months to find a wife and to stay married for three months. His granddaddy liked the three-month deadline. Why three months? He had no idea, but thank goodness it wasn't six months or a year to stay married.

He'd been determined to find someone to go along

with the scheme—marry him for three months and then get a nice fat reward package at the end. He'd thought he could go through with it like his granddaddy wanted. He'd get married and then at the end of the three-month term, they'd get a divorce. Simple and easy. She'd get her money and he'd regain his freedom and his ranch. The problem was, he hadn't found anyone willing to go along with the scheme. Well, he had found a few but then he'd not been able to go through with the offer…just hadn't been able to force himself to finalize the deal. And now he was on the verge of letting his entire family down, including his granddaddy with his crazy idea.

He'd stopped by this truck stop, blurry-eyed and depressed, trying to figure out what he was going to do. And now this sweet-looking, soft-spoken waitress was offering to take him up on this offer. She had a tragic story and was obviously desperate.

"You're seriously considering this?" he asked, feeling her desperation and feeling bad about even considering taking advantage of her desperation. But she wanted to do it and he had too much to gain to wimp out now. It was just so crazy. His granddaddy knew him, knew he wouldn't take kindly to being forced into doing something. But Wade knew this was a desperate act on Granddaddy's part because he wanted great-grandchildren on the ranch. Sadly, his granddaddy wanted this to save his legacy, but it wasn't going to do that. Wade wasn't going to stay married. He wasn't going to have children with whomever he married because of this will. But if he could marry someone, save the ranch, then he and she go their separate ways at the end of the ninety days, everything would be fine. And for the first time since he'd started looking for a short-term bride he felt he could go through with it. He felt compelled to go through with it.

Short-term.

Maybe one of his brothers would marry and carry the legacy on.

He watched her toy with the napkin in her hand that had been on the table for whoever sat on that side of the booth. Her pink tongue darted out and she licked her lips. She was nervous as she looked at him with

29

worried eyes.

"Well, it is a strange proposition, but yes…I think I could do that. If you're sure that at the end of three months it would be over and there's nothing romantic involved. I hate to say it, but the money is what I'm looking at. I could use that money desperately."

He reminded himself that he wasn't taking advantage of her. This was mutually beneficial for both of them. He could just give her the money and not the deal, but this wasn't just about him. It was about his brothers, too. Despite them telling him to not do it.

If he gave her the money and they didn't get married in three days, all his bank accounts would be frozen and he was going to have to start from scratch. That wasn't right. He had helped build that ranch. They had been partners, he thought. He had been there most of his life and had worked hard, put his blood and sweat into the place, and then he had put his education to work on it, too and the ranch was stronger because of him.

Reaching out, he covered her hand with his. "Allie, I know I just met you and that this is crazy…believe me, I believe it's crazy too, and I may be able to tell you the whole story later on, but not right now…yeah, the basics are just what you stated. We get married before Thursday, which would be the end of my three-month deadline to find a wife, and then I inherit my ranch and everything that comes with it as long as you stick with me for three months. No romance involved. You don't have to worry about that. You'll have your own room. Well, stipulations in the fine print of the will say we have to share a room, but you'll have your own room. Nobody else has to know about it. And, well, at the end of three months, we will go our separate ways and you will be taken care of, even if it's above and beyond what Granddaddy put in the will, which is very generous. There is a prenuptial agreement but it will be well worth your time."

She looked resolved, her big blue eyes bright with what he thought were threatening tears.

"Then I'm going to do this." Her voice wobbled. "You might not realize this, but you're an answered prayer for me. I've been worrying, I've been sick worrying and working so many hours with the knowledge that I'm not going to be able to make payments and get my mama the help she needs. So, I'll marry you. But I'm going to have to have some of that money upfront because I have a deadline, too. Monday, to be exact."

He was doing this. She needed him. "You've got a deal." He gently squeezed her hands, only then realizing he was still covering her hands with his. Her hand was warm and trembled. He felt the nervousness strumming through her. The need to protect her seized him. As he gently squeezed her hand, her deep blue eyes grew misty with tears.

"Thank you, Wade. Thank you. So, now what?"

From the back of the diner, the cook yelled out, "Order up!"

She sprang to her feet. "I have to go. I have to finish this shift. They're short-handed. Can you stick around? Can we meet tomorrow and figure this out?"

He stood. "Yeah, I'll find a room for the night and I'll meet you at the courthouse. Is there someplace near there where we can go over everything?"

"There is a park next to the courthouse. We could

meet there."

"I'll be there and if you still want to go through with it, I'll get a marriage license."

She agreed, and then he watched her hurry toward the back. "Allie," he called, and she spun around back toward him. "I hope this eases your mind. I promise it's going to be okay."

She gave a smile that sent a zing of electricity through him. She had a beautiful smile.

"I actually believe you. I'll be there. Is eight o'clock good?"

"Yes."

"Okay. And, Wade, I promise you, you won't be sorry. I'm not a quack. I just need the money. I won't give you any trouble."

He smiled at her, trying to reassure her because he could tell she was a ball of nerves. "And Allie, I give you my word that I won't give you any trouble either. You're in good hands, I promise. I'll be forever thankful to you."

They stared at each other, and he realized that those big blue eyes of hers were about the prettiest thing he ever did see, maybe just because she was doing him such a huge favor. At least, he decided as he walked out of the truck stop, he'd have something real pretty to look at for the next three months. That, at least, was a plus.

As he reached the parking lot, he looked up at the dark-blue sky and a sense of relief came over him. "Granddaddy, I don't know what you're up to, but this is going to happen. I'm not going to let you down. I sure hope somewhere along the way you tell me why in the Sam Hill you're putting me through this. I thought I was going to lose everything. I hope you're smiling up there now." With that, he got in his truck and headed down the road toward the hotel he had spotted from the highway. Tomorrow was the start of a new day.

Allie couldn't sleep. She was too excited and nervous, and she thought she was going to throw up, but she didn't. She got up and dressed early and looked around her little apartment and wondered what she was supposed to do next. *Did she pack?* Wherever she was going—she didn't even *know* where she was going. *This was crazy.* She calmed her nerves. She might be crazy, but this was her only chance of helping her mom, and she would do anything to help her mom. She thought about her poor daddy and having lost him, and the pain that she had felt, and then the knowledge that she didn't have him to rely on anymore. She relied completely on herself.

She would figure it out. She had to figure it out.

First, she better call Ginny. She was toast. Who was she kidding—when her best friend found out what she was planning…she was burnt toast. She picked up the phone and dialed her number.

"Hello." Ginny sounded as if she'd barely woke up.

"Ginny, are you awake?" she asked, despite the obvious.

"Yeah. I answered the phone, didn't I?" Ginny groaned into the phone. She was also a waitress at a diner in town, and she worked late. "Girl, what time is it?"

Allie laughed. "A little after seven. But oh, Ginny, I'm so nervous, I don't even know why or what I'm thinking. I had to call you."

Ginny suddenly sounded more alert. "Allie, what is going on? You sound strange. Are you all right? Is your mama okay?"

Her sweet friend was always looking out for her, and that was part of why she was nervous because she knew Ginny was going to be upset. "Relax, Ginny. Everything is okay. Mama is the same, but she's going to be fine because, well, I've agreed to something and it's going to mean that she is going to get everything she needs."

"How? What's happened? Did you win the lottery?"

Allie bit her lip and then went for it. "In a way, yes. Are you sitting down?"

"I'm in bed. What in the tarnation is going on? You don't gamble and you sound strange."

Allie took a deep breath. "Okay, so...I'm getting married."

"What!"

The shriek over the phone practically burst Allie's eardrums. She held the phone away from her ear for a second and then prepared herself for battle.

"What's going on? *You don't even date.* How can you be getting married? Have you been keeping something from me?"

"No, Ginny. I have not been keeping anything from you. You'd have tortured it out of me anyways if I was trying to keep something from you. That's why I'm calling you. Look, this cowboy came by the truck stop last night. He looked real sad."

A groan came from the other end of the line. "Please don't tell me that you fell for another sob story from another stinkin' cowboy. What is up with every loser cowboy out there finding you and—"

"Ginny, wait, slow down. It was *kind* of a sob story, but it's very unique." Her friend tried to start up again. "Halt. Hold your horses and don't talk for a minute, okay? Promise? This is not like the-one-who-will-not-be-named."

Ginny growled then heaved a sigh. "I promise. Just tell me what in the tarnation is going on."

"Okay, he has to get married by the end of the day—by Thursday, actually—or else he loses his big ranch, his inheritance. At least, it sounds like a big ranch from the way he's talking about it. His granddaddy stipulated this in his will, and he obviously likes three-month markers. Obviously, he goes by quarters. I'm sorry, I'm rambling, but if we stay married for three months, then I get money for marrying him right up front, but it's not the big money. I get that if I stay married to him for three months. And there's not going to be any hanky-panky going on. No romance. I just have to stay married to him for three months because if he gets married, he saves his ranch for him and his brothers. If he doesn't get married, even his brothers lose out on the inheritance, and I don't know who gets the ranch if that happens. But just remember, I'm getting something out of this. I'm getting enough money in the beginning to pay for my mama's rehab and hopefully she will come out of the coma."

"This sounds way too fishy."

"I know, but if you'd been there and heard him—

seen him—you'd see why I believe him. He said I would get plenty of money to take care of my mama. And this morning, I'm meeting him at the park across from the courthouse to go over the contract and the prenuptial contract. Then we're going to the clerk's office where we're going to get our marriage license. Whew! I am so nervous."

Tension-filled silence was all she heard from the other end of the phone line.

"Ginny, are you still there?"

"I am here," Ginny gritted out through what sounded like clenched teeth.

Allie prepared herself for what was about to happen. This was the calm before the storm. Before the deluge hit like a Texas flash flood. She'd known this from the beginning.

"Allie, you are too sweet and have always been gullible. Your heart is too good. But this time that sweet heart of yours has gone way off the deep end. I cannot believe how low this guy is willing to go to get—to get a woman. *Geesh*."

"It's not like that."

"How do you know that you are truly going to get this money? Did you ask for credentials? Did you ask for some form of ID? What do you know about this guy? I'm getting dressed right now. Do not go meet this guy at that courthouse. You could go missing. He's a creep. He could be taking you off and I will never see you again. You will never see anyone again. You will probably disappear. Allie, I cannot believe you're doing this."

"Ginny, Ginny, calm down! *Ginny*, calm down!"

"*Ouch!* Darn it."

Allie cringed, listening. It sounded as if she were hopping around as she probably tried to pull on her ever-present jeans on one leg at a time and running into things as she did so.

"I am not going to calm down. *Ouch*—I am telling you, Allie, I am going to be there in five minutes." There was a crash. "*Ouch. For Pete's sake.* Well, it might be longer than that. Don't you go anywhere."

"Ginny, I'm supposed to meet him at little before eight. It will take me ten minutes to get down there. I have to leave now. I don't want to make him wait. I'm going to do this."

"I will be at that park. You are not marrying this jerk. You got that?"

Allie groaned. She had known it was going to be bad, but not this bad. All she needed was Ginny the *Warrior-Sister* to come up there and mess everything up. "Ginny, please calm down. I need this. I don't need you coming up there and messing everything up. Please, please, listen to me. He is a *nice* guy, I can tell."

"*Excuse me*? Did you forget all the times that you have been so gullible with men who have taken advantage of you? Like that time that—"

"Please don't go there. Please. I am not being gullible, I promise you. I sat down and I had a nice conversation with him. He is not like those other guys. Especially not like *him*."

"You are too important to me, girlfriend. I'm going to meet him. I'm not letting you do this. I will meet you at the courthouse in ten minutes. And whoever this guy is, he better be ready, because I am coming with all my barrels firing."

"Please don't bring Loretta." Allie rubbed her forehead.

"Oh, you can bet I'm bringing Loretta. Best backup a girl can have."

Allie had a headache, but she also had a deadline. She grabbed her purse and tucked her phone in her pocket because Ginny had hung up on her and was probably yanking on the rest of her clothes. Who knew—she might be in her pajamas when she arrived. There was no telling what was about to happen when Ginny arrived. But one thing was for sure—she needed Ginny for backup. This was a major decision and Ginny had more experience with contracts. She just needed to prepare Wade for what was coming. Because when Ginny was mad, she was worse than a Texas tornado.

The-one-who-shall-not-be-named had wished he'd never met her. And, well, Ginny sounded madder now than then. Ginny had found Allie and *him* in his hotel room just in the nick of time. Allie had managed to lock herself in the bathroom...she didn't even want to think about it. But Ginny had saved her that night. That cowboy had been coming by the truck stop a lot and had been flirting with her and trying to get her to go out with him. She'd said no every time he asked but he wasn't getting the hint. Then he'd started telling her how sick his grandmother was. She'd felt really bad for him. When he'd told her he needed help getting her to the hospital, Allie had gone with him. Stupid, stupid mistake. Even more stupid: when they reached the hotel room and she'd let him convince her that his grandma was inside. Yeah, right—the Big Bad Wolf was in there. Thankfully, she'd texted Ginny and told her the room number. Ginny had arrived with Loretta—her pink, double-barreled shotgun—in tow. Thank goodness.

She had gone to help his grandma. Yeah, she knew that sounded pretty lame, but this was different. She could feel that it was different. Wade's steady, serious eyes filled her mind. He couldn't be a jerk. He just couldn't be.

Ginny had saved her before. But never had it been that serious. Her friend had ridden to her rescue with those barrels blazing, shot that doorknob off that hotel room and found *him* in his underwear, picking the lock on the bathroom door.

All Allie had heard was a lot of begging going on until Ginny had told her to come out of the bathroom. The cowboy had gone willingly with the cops, screaming to get him away from the crazy woman.

Thinking of those barrels, Allie raced to her car. She had to get to the courthouse, and she had to get there now to warn Wade what was coming.

CHAPTER THREE

Wade was pacing in the small park when he saw Allie drive up in her very old Corolla. He halted, then shifted his weight from one boot to the other as he watched her get out of the car. She hesitated for a moment as their gazes met. She pushed her hair away from her face, looking pensive. He'd struggled all night about doing this. She seemed very sweet, but very vulnerable. He was worried. He had told himself over and over again that he wasn't taking advantage of her. But it felt as if he were because she was desperate to help her mother.

But he was desperate too.

As she started toward him, his gut clenched. She wore jeans and a blue top. With her hair pulled back in a ponytail, she looked younger than she had last night in the brown truck-stop uniform. Her jeans were rolled at the ankles and she had on flat-footed Converse tennis shoes that he had seen mostly teenagers wearing. Maybe the weariness on her face last night had aged her. She still looked tired, and her big, blue eyes that dominated her face were full of worry. The closer she got, the younger she looked.

He groaned. *How old was this woman?*

The minute she got to him, he didn't waste any time. "Okay, first things first—how old are you? I didn't ask you last night, but today you look really young."

She looked panicked. "I'm twenty-four years old. I just look young for my age. It's been a curse all my life. But don't worry, I'm plenty old. I've had two years of college...and I have my driver's license if you don't believe me. It's in the car. I can go get it."

She spun to go back and he reached out and

grabbed her arm. Her skin was soft and warmth raced through him. "Wait…I believe you."

She closed her eyes as if saying a prayer of thanks. Desperation clung to her. "Good. How old are you?"

"I'm twenty-nine, going on thirty in just a few months. I just needed to make sure you were older than you looked. I need to know I'm not taking advantage of you."

She smiled and his pulse raced. "I understand."

"And I have to tell you, probably if you were much younger than twenty-four, I wouldn't be able to do this anyway. I have to make sure you're old enough to really understand what you're doing."

She looked indignant. "Look, I may be a little vulnerable and that's what I'm trying to tell you, but I understand what I'm doing. I understand completely what I'm doing. I am not stupid. But I need to tell you something. My friend…"

His attention turned completely to the Jeep that had just whirled into the parking lot next to her Corolla. A woman wearing a cowboy hat sat in the open-air Jeep. She immediately sprang from the Jeep and started fast-walking toward them. She looked seriously like she wanted to hurt someone.

Him.

"Who—"

"That's what I was trying to tell you. That's my friend Ginny. And she's really mad and she…she's coming here, and she's going to get you. I mean…I'm sorry…she's going to try and stop you. She's really protective of me."

Before she could get anything else out, the gal in the cowboy hat had reached them. She skidded to a halt in front of him. She was pretty. She had curly brown hair and a sassy look about her. She wore a Western shirt and her jeans were tucked into her cowboy boots. Her hat was beat up, one of those that gals bought at the dime store or the convenience store or the truck stop. It was a play hat, but he guessed that it was one of those designer things, he thought. He figured she wasn't a real cowgirl, but that she liked to dress like one. She was hot. She was hot but he meant hot, like mad hot. There was practically steam coming out of her ears.

"Okay, buster." She jabbed a finger in his chest. "Just what do you think you're doing? Because if you think you're going to con my friend into marrying you, you've got another thing coming. You are not going to get to her today. You just take your lies and whatever else you've been spilling and you just get in your truck and you hightail it out of here."

"Ginny, please…this is Wade McCoy. And he's not spilling me lies. I told you, he's nice."

She thought he was nice. Wade stared at Ginny. He couldn't get mad because he admired her. She had spunk, and she was trying to protect Allie. He liked that. He figured that anyone as sweet-looking and sweet-acting as Allie probably needed someone to protect her. Heck, *he* wanted to protect her. He couldn't help himself. From the moment he saw her, he wanted to protect her. When he walked into that truck stop last night, his first thought was that she looked tired and he wished she could sit down. Then he got lost in his own worries and thoughts.

"Ginny, it's good to meet you, and I can show you my credentials. I am not trying to take advantage of your friend. I need her help and she needs my help. I promise, it's going to be okay." It was; he would make sure of it.

Ginny's eyes drilled into him. "And you can bet I want to see those credentials. I want to know who you are. I want to see a contract. You know, write something down that says that she isn't obligated to you for anything and that she's getting what you say she's getting. I am not her keeper, but, I can't help but make sure she's okay."

He glanced at Allie. She was pink and biting her bottom lip. He had to fight the desire to wrap his arm around her and tell her everything was going to be okay.

"I contacted my lawyer last night and he faxed me the contracts. I have all the paperwork right here." He pointed to where he had a briefcase on the table. He strode over, snapped the leather case open, and pulled out all the paperwork. He handed it to Allie. "Everything's written out in there. I'm glad you've got a friend with you to look it over. If you want to take it to a lawyer to look over, that's fine...if he can do it this morning. You read it and tell me if the money is enough." He knew he was leaving himself open for vulnerability, but he was desperate and he wanted to believe that this sweet-faced woman was what she said she was and wasn't going to try to take advantage of him.

"Thank you. Ginny, come on." Allie headed to the end of the table and sat down.

Ginny stepped over the bench seat and sat down beside her.

Wade moved away. He wanted to pace, but he knew that would make them nervous, so he walked over to a tree and turned his back to lean against it, with his book propped open. He waited. Several minutes later, after the two had their heads bent over the papers and talked together over various pages, Allie waved him over.

Ginny watched him and seemed more subdued, and that was good.

"Ginny and I have looked at this and we agree that it looks good. I'm not a lawyer or anything, so I'm going to trust you on some of this that it's the truth. So,

I'm going to sign it."

Ginny stared at him. "She's going to sign it because I agree with her. It all looks above board. But if she calls me and she needs me, I do have a gun and I am going to come see you."

He smiled at her. He took her threat to be the truth. He had a feeling that she did have a gun and she did know how to use it. Heck, most women in Texas did. He tried to reassure her anyways. "I promise, you are not going to have to come see me with your gun. I will be a gentleman. I will honor what's in that contract, and at the end of three months, Allie can walk away a richer woman."

"And no monkey business." Ginny gave him the evil eye.

"Ginny, *stop*." Allie gave her friend a pleading look then gave him an apologetic one. "Wade, like I said last night, you're the answer to my prayers. And Ginny, she's always been my protector ever since we were little kids, so you'll have to forgive her. She wouldn't shoot you—although I won't say she wouldn't shoot someone who was trying to hurt me.

She might kick you where it hurts, but she wouldn't shoot *you*."

He grimaced. "I promise you, she's not going to have to kick me either."

Ginny hiked a brow. "Hope not."

One thing was certain: Allie had one vigilant, slightly scary friend in her corner. The fact made him feel good for Allie.

Allie and Ginny had spent the evening packing her things that she would take to Wade's Hill Country ranch on the outskirts of Fredericksburg. Ginny was resigned that she was going through with the wedding but after exhaustive research on Wade McCoy, everything was clearer now. He was very rich. So rich she couldn't even fathom his wealth. The McCoy fortune was estimated in the billions. *Billions.*

With Ginny as her witness, Allie stood in front of the justice of the peace and exchanged wedding vows the next day. She stared into Wade's earnest eyes and butterflies swirled inside her. He was so handsome and he seemed so nice and there was a chemistry she felt humming between them...on her part, anyway. But she had to keep reminding herself this was strictly a business deal. Absolutely nothing else mattered. And then there was her track record with men that was not the most reliable. She inhaled sharply as he took her hands and the JP recited the vows. Fake vows. Not the real vows she longed for one day. This was not that day. This was for her mother.

She was still trying to figure out why Wade's granddaddy would threaten to give away his legacy instead of willing it to the grandsons who loved him and had worked beside him to build his fortune and legacy on the ranch Wade obviously loved. She didn't believe it was all about the money.

Allie was thankful Ginny had come around. They had talked late into the night as they packed up most of her clothes and got her ready for this trip. She called and apologized to her boss at the truck stop for having to leave him on such short notice. She felt bad, but there was nothing else she could do. He was a nice guy and she had worked for him off and on through the years, started when she was in college and then before she opened her florist shop and then recently when she needed a job so desperately. As always, he told her she was a good waitress and that if she ever needed a job, she had one at the truck stop. He had always given her a job when she needed one and she would forever be grateful to him.

As she looked into Wade McCoy's face and he slipped the simple gold band on her finger, and that justice of the peace pronounced them man and wife, she prayed that things were going to be okay. Her mother would have the care she needed and she would have funds to start over when the three months were up. Things did seem brighter. Hopefully Wade was as good of a guy as she thought he was and she had nothing to fear.

But as he slipped that ring onto her finger, that needling little hope, that little wish that she had always had for getting married and having the perfect little white house with the white picket fence and a house full of babies too…kindled like a small flame inside her.

Stop.

She yanked her thoughts from such a ridiculous dream. This handsome cowboy was her knight in shining armor but he was not her Prince Charming. He was not the man of her dreams; he was just the man of the moment who had ridden to her rescue. And soon he would be riding away.

The best thing she could do going into this was to not let herself feel any romantic notions toward him. But as he leaned forward, his eyes all serious and compelling, butterflies filled her stomach. The moment his lips touched hers, though as briefly as a feather, she felt a tiny flame in her stomach. It was a flame she had never felt before.

When Wade pulled back, she felt dazed, despite the briefness of his lips touching hers. It left her head spinning as realization hit that despite her best intentions, she might be in trouble.

CHAPTER FOUR

By the time they were headed down the highway toward Stonewall, the closest town to his ranch in Hill Country, she knew it would be beautiful. Anything near the Guadalupe River would be beautiful. Texas Hill Country was gorgeous anyway, with a medley of landscapes from rivers to rocky hills and cliffs overlooking valleys where several rivers meandered through the counties on their way to the Gulf.

Once, as a child, they'd vacationed on the Guadalupe and she could still remember how cold the water was when they'd climbed into their inner tubes and floated leisurely downstream. It was one of her best memories of her family. Her throat ached as she thought of it and she focused on the passing landscape and tried not to cry. Instantly, her thoughts switched to Wade's brief kiss. Her lips were still warm from it. Her tears dried up but she told herself not to think about that. This was a non-romantic situation that she was in. It was all about the money—all about the money and the land. This was only about three months of her life and that according to that contract, he had stated very clearly that the marriage would be over.

"Don't you let that man into your heart," Ginny had told her. *"Because you know you'll get burned."*

Ginny had been very blunt, and Allie knew that Ginny was right. Ginny had seen her when she had been vulnerable. Ginny had always been her protector, which was ridiculous. She didn't need a protector. She wanted to stand on her own two feet. She wanted to make her own decisions where men were concerned, but she was such a tender heart.

Looking out the window, she watched the miles go by. When Wade continued to be silent, she shot him a quick glance. He was watching the road. He had one hand on the steering wheel at eight o'clock and one hand on the steering wheel at two o'clock. His hat was pulled low over his forehead and he looked as if he were deep in thought. He was so handsome, so wealthy... It hit her suddenly that she would not fit into his world. Not even for three months.

She'd been so wrapped up in helping her mother and getting this done that it hadn't clearly sank in that she'd just married a billionaire. No way would she know the first thing about fitting into his life.

Her heart thundered; she leaned her head to the side and rested her forehead on her hand, using it to shield her eyes slightly as she pretended to be asleep. If he thought she was asleep, then there was no awkwardness on her part riding here with him not talking. Or her not talking either. She closed her eyes and tried hard not to feel as though she wasn't good enough.

It wasn't a new feeling, so why, she wondered, did it suddenly hurt so much?

Wade had been lost in thought most of the trip, and he was kind of thankful Allie was sleeping because he had been disturbed ever since the wedding. Ever since the justice of the peace announced that they were man and wife and he had kissed her. All he could think about was that when his lips touched hers, he felt as if he stood in the middle of a grass fire in the prairie, and he was all burned up. It was a terrible analogy, but the office got hot, and he had to fight the notion to wrap his arms around her, pull her tight, and deepen the kiss. They had chemistry. He reminded himself that at the end of three months, she wasn't going to be his wife anymore and he had promised her he was not taking advantage of her. There would be no romance.

He'd thought it wasn't going to be that hard of a thing, but then...that kiss. The kiss to end all kisses had happened and now things were a lot murkier than they had been.

He pulled into a convenience store parking lot for a restroom break and to fill up the tank. He climbed from the truck and wanted to shout up at heaven and his granddaddy and yell, *"What were you thinking?"* But, he didn't. Instead, he turned back to look at Allie across the truck seat. He pushed down all of the emotions swamping him and then leaned in and gently touched Allie's shoulder.

"Hey, hey—you still sleeping? Thought you might want to get up and go to the ladies' room. I had to get gas, so I thought we might as well stop too. We still have about an hour to go before we reach the ranch. We'll stop to eat before we get there. There's a Mexican restaurant in Dripping Springs I thought we'd eat at. They have the best fajitas I've ever eaten, but their enchiladas there are really good, too. I'm a sucker for good Tex-Mex. I usually stop there every trip when I leave the ranch."

She blinked at him and he knew he was rambling. She hadn't said anything. She just stared back at him. Her blue eyes had a tinge of worry in them, he thought. Of course, he knew it was going to take a few days to get used to what they had done. It wasn't every day that you got married to a perfect stranger. To a girl like Allie, it probably wasn't even something that she had thought about, much less actually happened.

"Whatever you want. Sounds good. I think I will go inside. I might get me a cup of coffee too."

He reached in his pocket and yanked out a hundred-dollar bill. "Here, whatever you need. I might get me a cup of coffee, too."

She stared at the money. "Well, I could have gotten it, but thanks. Do you want me to get your coffee for you? I drink mine with two sugars and two creams. How do you drink yours?"

She looked like a sweet coffee drinker. "That'd be great. I drink mine black, straight up."

"Okay. I kind of figured that."

Without another word, she climbed out of the truck. His big Ford was a pretty good size, and she had to use the running board to get out by herself. He moved to the gas pump and turned to watch her as she walked across the pavement toward the store. Her shoulders were slumped and her hips swayed gently as her blonde hair kept rhythm. He groaned. She was cute. She was pretty. He yanked his gaze off her and turned back to the gas pump. *Kiss or no kiss, this was strictly a business deal.*

That thought in mind, he pushed his card into the gas pump's card reader then punched the buttons with the force of a right hook as he answered all the questions the gadget asked him. Finally, he grabbed the nozzle, rammed it into his gas tank and pumped gas into the tank.

His shoulders ached from the tension and frustration. And it was all Granddaddy's fault.

Fifteen minutes later, they were traveling back down the road. He was drinking his black coffee, and she was sipping on her sweet and creamy concoction. And, they weren't talking. They'd barely spoken the whole trip. She had slept most of the way. He was beginning to wonder whether she didn't sleep at night or something. Of course, he hadn't slept much last night either.

"Are you doing okay? I mean, you haven't asked many questions."

"I'm fine, but I will admit that I am a little nervous and unsure of myself. But once we get there, I'm sure I'll figure out what I'm supposed to do and how I'm supposed to act."

"You don't have to do anything, and you just need to act like yourself. I'm not expecting anything out of you. I'm getting what I need, which is just the ranch and my money for myself and my brothers. You should just look at this as a vacation. I mean, you look like you could use a little vacation, get some rest and relax. You look really tired and you've been sleeping the last four hours."

"I-I am tired. I didn't sleep at all last night. But a vacation? I'm going to be there for three months. I can't take a three-month vacation. I can't even take a one-week vacation. I need to be doing something or else I'll go stir-crazy. I'm just going to tell you that right now. I mean, really, Wade, you can't expect me to go there and not do something. I could clean house?"

He hadn't thought about this part. "We have a housekeeper. Nelda. She's the wife of the foreman,

Roland. She comes in every day and makes sure everything is looking good then cooks food so I'll have something when I come in from work. If you clean house, then she'll feel like she doesn't have a job to do."

"Oh, okay." Allie's expression tensed. "This is just so weird," she muttered under her breath.

He heard her comment and it made him smile. "Allie, we'll figure something out. Really, it's going to be fine. I mean, we're going to be on a ranch. If you want to work, there is always something to do on a ranch. Truth be told, you can get up before sunrise and go to bed after dark and still not get everything done. It's a big ranch. There are cows, lots of horses. There's a lot of calves and foals. There's a lot of crops too. We have a very large peach orchard. Hill Country is known for its peaches but many consider the Stonewall peaches to be the best and we have our share of them."

"Really? I had no idea you had all of that on your ranch. How big of a ranch are we talking about?" She took a sip of her coffee and then cleared her throat. "I'm sorry, I didn't mean to pry. You don't have to answer that."

"It's fine. We have land all over Texas but here we have several thousand acres. We aren't as big as the King Ranch, mind you, but Granddaddy and his brother were ambitious, so there's a bunch. They used to be very competitive in growing their land and fortunes. To be honest, I'm still doing an audit on what all Granddaddy bought recently. He bought things sight unseen at times but kept meticulous records, most of the time. Other times, not so great, so I'm finding surprises—more land than he even told me about. But anyway, about finding you something to do—we can do it."

"It all sounds very complicated. Maybe you can find something simple for me to do. I could pick peaches."

"We'll figure something out. Are you ready to eat?" The Mexican restaurant was just off the highway.

"Sure."

He pulled right into the parking lot and hurried around to her side. He went to pull the door open for her, but she had already done it and slid onto the ground from the truck.

She stretched. "I am starving."

He smiled at her, liking how easy she was to get along with. He realized he'd just told her his business. That he'd let his guard down with her and he never did that with a woman. He'd learned early on what he had was what they were after and it wasn't his good heart.

"Me too. But I promise you will like this place."

A few minutes later, they were seated at a booth in the corner. He ordered sweet tea and she ordered unsweetened tea.

He laughed. "We are opposites when it comes to our drinks. I'm no sweet on coffee and sweet on tea. You're sweet on coffee and unsweet on tea."

She laughed. "How about chips? Do you like salted or unsalted?"

"Salted."

"Whew, then we're safe on sharing chips because we finally agree on something." She picked the saltshaker up and gave the corn tortillas a liberal dusting of salt.

"In that case, I think we're going to be just fine."

They smiled at each other. Each grabbed a chip and dipped it in the salsa.

She bit into her chip and they spent the next few minutes digging in.

"So, tell me, Wade, with all that you have going on at the ranch, what is your favorite part? Oh wait, I know that you love it all. But, I mean, what is your favorite? What really gets your heart ticking the most?"

Wade stopped eating and stared at Allie. Her big eyes searched his and she leaned forward with her elbows on the table, clearly interested in what he was about to say.

"I…" He started to answer her, then just stared at her and shook his head. "You really want to know?"

She looked incredulous then smiled widely as her eyes danced. "I do. Surely something is your favorite."

"I love roundups. I love feeling like I've been thrown back in time just a little when we sleep in bedrolls underneath the starlit sky and listen to the cattle mooing occasionally and the crickets serenading and the wild calls of coyotes in the distance.

Granddaddy loved that the most too." He smiled at Allie as a sudden lump formed in his throat. He swallowed hard. "As wealthy as he was, he went on as many roundups as he could. We were on one just a couple of days before he died."

He'd rested his hand on the table beside the basket of chips that were now forgotten. Allie's soft, warm hand covered his and their gazes met. And he felt suddenly that she understood.

Her pretty lips quirked upward. "It's hard. But he left you with a lot of good memories. My dad did too. But…" She sighed. "I still miss him. I'm glad you're not losing your ranch."

What did he say to that? "Me too. Thanks to you."

CHAPTER FIVE

When they drove onto the land that was the ranch that belonged to Wade now, Allie was completely zoned in on it. Her curiosity about her new husband and his family was piqued, and she couldn't help but be curious. It was beautiful. It was the land of Hill Country. Yaupon trees and bluebonnets were scattered throughout the pastures. There were the hills of the cliffs that ran along the edge of the river in the distance, and it was beautiful. It was different than other areas of Texas that she had been through. She had seen pictures of it before, but she had never actually been to this area. Texas was a big state.

The drive down through the pastures was white gravel. It had obviously been hauled down here, and the view was nice.

When the house came into view, she had to bite back a gasp.

As if reading her thoughts, Wade said, "My granddaddy built this for my grandmother about twenty years ago. It's bigger than I wanted, but I'm used to it now. Hopefully you'll be comfortable here. And like I said, you'll have your own room because there are a lot of bedrooms in this house."

"Yes, I see what you mean. It's huge. Sprawling, I guess, would be the word."

He laughed. "Sprawling. Yeah, that would be the word." He pulled into the yard and parked.

She hopped out of the truck, not waiting for him to come around and open the door for her. He had tried earlier to come and open her door, but she had beat him then too. She just wasn't used to that and she didn't want to get used to it.

He strode around the truck and put his hands on

his hips. "Beat me again."

"Sorry."

His smile caused her pulse to hum. "Come on, I'll show you to your room and I'll bring your suitcases in later. I know you're tired and you probably want to get a little rest."

"True, but I mean, I'm not just going to fall asleep on you when we walk in the door."

He laughed. "Well, let's play it by ear. This late, it's just going to be the two of us in there anyway."

The house was huge. One of those very Western inspired, masculine homes with big vaulted ceilings and huge beams. The fireplace in the main room was massive. As was the staircase to the second floor and the kitchen was straight out of a magazine.

"This is amazing."

Wade turned and took in the room. "Yeah, it's something. A bit cavernous with just me here. When we were kids, it was different. I used to ride that banister down several times a day. My brothers, too. Granddaddy loved it."

She imagined him sliding down the banister. It

was very high and dangerous, and she had a feeling he said "Yeehaw" a few times on the way down. She smiled. "If I were a mother, it would terrify me."

"My mom would have agreed with you."

When Wade showed her to the room that would be hers, it was across the hall from his room. He told her that they'd put her things in his room, but that they'd have different sleeping arrangements and nobody needed to know.

It was kind of awkward at first, him talking about that, but she just wished for the morning to go better. This was going to be awkward—there was no way around it. But oddly enough, she trusted him. She had trusted him from the very beginning. So, he brought all her things in and he placed them in his room. Then, she got her stuff out of her bag that she needed, took a shower, and climbed into the big bed. Her body sank into the plush mattress and she sighed. "What a day."

She had really gotten married. Really written the rehabilitation facility a check to cover getting her mother transferred in and now she was here. She'd gone by to see her mother before the wedding, not that her mother was awake or could know her. But she had been to the hospital every day since the accident and now she would call every day because she couldn't physically go by. She felt terrible about not being there, but if she hadn't married Wade, her mother wouldn't get the care she needed. Wade had said he would have her flown in to see her at any time. She had done everything she could do for now.

And all because of Wade McCoy, her husband. The past two days were crazy and unbelievable. But as she lay there thinking about tomorrow, excitement filled her. She was going to look at this with a positive outlook. And she was trying really hard to enjoy herself for the short time she was here…and she was going to believe with all her heart that her mother was going to pull out of this coma.

The next morning, Wade rose early and went out to the barn to check on his animals.

Clay, his friend and top hand, sauntered into the barn. "Morning, boss," he drawled and grinned. "I see you made it back. Did you find any new stock out there at that stock show for us?"

"I did. There were some really good bulls. They'll be delivered here next week, so you'll need to get ready."

"Oh, we're ready. We've got it all figured out. We've got the breeding schedules lined up."

"Good. Clay, I got married. I brought my bride back with me."

At his blunt words, Clay squinted at him. "Say what?"

"You heard me. I got married. So, I just want to pre-warn you, and maybe you can spread the word while y'all are out working cows, that my wife is now living at the big house. Her name is Allie. She's great."

"I didn't even know you were dating anybody."

"I wasn't, but well, you know the stipulations to the will, and you know that my time was about out." Not everybody on the ranch knew the details of the will, but Clay was his closest friend aside from his brothers, so he knew. And Clay knew that things were desperate.

"Wow, you did it. I don't know how you convinced her to get married, but I should have believed in you all along."

"I thought I wasn't going to be able to do it, but Allie had her own reasons and agreed to help me out."

Clay's eyes narrowed with wariness. "What kind of a person is she to agree to this?"

"She's a good person. She's a real good person. She was just in a predicament. We were brought together by fate. I'm giving her what she needed, and she's giving me what I needed."

"I'm stunned. Happy for you and all of us wranglers to keep our jobs. How did Todd and Morgan take the news?"

"Haven't told them yet. Only people who know are you, Nelda, and the lawyer. I'll call them later today and tell them. But they're going to be glad."

At least he figured they would be, despite their aggravation at their granddad forcing this on him.

Allie woke and ignored the trepidation curling in her

stomach. She dressed quickly, still trying to get used to the beauty of the room she was in and the weirdness that in some ways, she was camping out in this room. Wade had explained to her that there was no stipulation that they had to consummate the marriage but they were supposed to be sharing a room. He truly had no idea whether there was some kind of stipulation in his granddaddy's will that there would be someone dropping in to check on the room status. At this point, he didn't know what to expect from his granddaddy, he'd said, so therefore, he wanted to be safe and make it appear that they were following every detail of the contract.

Allie thought that Wade's grandfather sounded desperate. She agreed with Wade that he was trying to help Wade fall in love and that three months probably would be enough for two people to find out whether they were or not. She thought it was all very weird, but she also admired Mr. McCoy for trying to help his grandson find a wife, or better yet, someone to share his life with. They'd both speculated that maybe he thought if you were incompatible within three months, that it probably wasn't happening. She just hoped that she and Wade were compatible enough to live in the same house together for three months. She envisioned Ginny in this situation, and she didn't think whoever the guy was would be able to last. Not unless there was a strong connection because Ginny was her own person and either you loved her, or you didn't. That would have made something like this really awkward and hard. She laughed thinking about it. But of course, this would never happen to Ginny. That girl would never agree to something so crazy. And besides, her parents had the winery and she was indispensable to them.

Gathering her things, Allie looked around the room and made sure it looked like it did before she slept there. Then she peeked out the door and then snuck into the hallway to Wade's room. He had told her to just go inside, that he would be up early and down at the stables or in his office and that if she needed him, those would be the places to find him. That breakfast would be downstairs, and she would probably be able to find Nelda in the kitchen. Now, she opened his bedroom door, feeling weird going inside his room. He had shown her the closet last night briefly, and said he would clean out some space for her in the dresser and that there was plenty of space in the walk-in closet for her things. He hadn't been wrong. It was massive.

Glancing around his room, feeling intrusive but curious, she was struck again by how beautiful it was. It was large, masculine, and the tan and red theme that was going on was subtle but nice. It clearly said that Wade had no female in his life. There was a lot of leather in the seating area next to a fireplace in the room. There were double doors leading out onto a private patio. It was a truly wonderful room, and she envisioned it with warmer tones and a more romantic touch to it. *Stop.* She shouldn't be thinking things like that because she was not here to stay.

Unable to help herself, she walked over to the double doors and opened them. Stepping out onto the patio, she took in the view. The house sat on a sloped piece of land, so that there were steps leading from the patio to the gradual sloping hillside. She could see ranchland and the river in the distance. It was beautiful and it was dotted with both dove-gray cattle and black cattle. Maybe Brahman or Brangus, Texas breeds she'd often heard talked about…though she couldn't really tell you what they were—the kind that had some kind of hump on their backs? What she saw in Wade's pasture had a hump at their shoulders.

She was, she decided, going to get an education about ranching while she was here. Something she'd never really had any reason to wonder about before. She caught movement out of the corner of her eye and focused on the buildings. A barn and then what she believed was the stable. Wade was talking to a couple of cowboys. He looked no different than the other two men from this distance but despite not being able to see his face, she was surprised that she could recognize him from this distance simply by the way he stood and the way he carried himself when he walked. He had his hat pulled low. He had on worn jeans, creased down the front—even from this distance, she could tell that they were pressed. They looked as if they were velvety to the touch, which they weren't; it was just that they were well-worn and that they were probably starched and creased their entire life and the starch was probably burned into them, giving them that appearance. It was a common look of cowboys who could afford to have someone do their laundry every day. Not everyone could afford that, and not every cowboy had that, so she should have guessed that there was something to him the first time she saw him enter the truck stop. She'd been too busy to notice small details like that, though.

Still, nothing about his appearance then or now gave her a clue that Wade McCoy was a billionaire cowboy. The man had stopped to get coffee at the highway truck stop, for heaven's sake.

Something drew his attention and he glanced about as if searching. Then it seemed as if he looked directly at her. She could feel his eyes on her and her heart raced instantly. He verified that he saw her when he lifted his hand in acknowledgment then tipped his hat at her. Feeling crazily breathless, she lifted her hand and gave a small wave, feeling very awkward and uncertain. He now knew that she had been in his room and that she had been on his patio. There was a wall beside the patio that gave this section some semblance of privacy from the rest of the house. If she had just stayed back closer to the doors a little bit, he would never have known she had been out there. But no, she had left the house and walked to the edge of the patio so that she was in full view of anyone who was out there. She told herself not to be self-conscious as she turned and headed back into the room and carefully closed the doors. He had given her permission to be where she was, and that was all that this was. She was just exploring.

But it was his own private area and that was why it felt so intrusive to her. She was married to him but not a part of this...not as if they were a real happily married couple.

She left the bedroom and headed back the way they had come the night before until she found herself back in the large kitchen. A woman of about fifty was in the kitchen. She had short blonde hair and a trim figure in jeans and boots and a colorful T-shirt. She spun the moment she heard Allie enter the kitchen.

"Good morning, Allie." A warm smile lifted the edges of her eyes and the suntanned skin crinkled from her cheeks to the edges of her eyes. "I'm Nelda, Wade's housekeeper. And I am so happy to say congratulations to you. Wade told me you two got married yesterday. I'm very excited. I just want you to know that if you ever need anything, you just let me know. I'm married to the foreman—I'm sure he's told you that. Roland has been the foreman on this ranch for a long time. I can tell you he's going to be thrilled, too. He and Wade's granddad were great friends and he's always said that J.D.—that's Mr. McCoy's first name, in case you didn't know—always wanted his boys married. This ranch is a wonderful place to live and bring up a family."

Nelda was about her own mother's age and Allie liked her on the spot but wondered whether she knew about the will. "Thank you. I'm excited to look around. I'm going to go exploring here in just a little while, but I thought I'd grab a cup of coffee."

Nelda immediately turned toward the coffeemaker, grabbed a red mug off a mug rack, and filled it with coffee. "Coffee will be here any time you want it, and cream and sugar too. I set it out for you since Wade told me that you liked them both in your coffee. Anything you need, just look in the pantry or the fridge and if you don't find what you want, just tell me and I'll pick it up at the grocery store. Also, there's bacon and eggs on the stove. Or I can make you an omelet or pancakes if you prefer. If you'd like homemade biscuits, they're in the oven. I can fix you up a plate."

This was overwhelming, to say the least. Allie was the one who waited on people, not the other way around. "Um, that's very nice of you. I'll just take a piece of bacon, but I'm really not hungry at the moment. I think I'm going to head down to the barn, but I'll take my bacon and my coffee. And I'll have one of those biscuits when I get back." She didn't want to hurt Nelda's feelings considering she'd gone to all this trouble.

"That's great. Everything will be in the oven on warm. Do you need any help unpacking or anything like that?"

Again, Allie wasn't sure how much Nelda knew about her and Wade's marriage. Did she know it was just so that he would keep the inheritance in the family? She decided that Nelda didn't need to know if at all possible. "No, thank you, I can do it, but it's really nice meeting you. I'm sure that I'll settle in nicely."

Nelda smiled warmly. "I hope so. I am just thrilled as peach pie to have you here."

Allie realized, as awkward as everything felt, that she was glad to be here too. But for the first time since marrying Wade, she felt the tug of guilt at not being completely truthful about their situation. What would Nelda think about her when she found out that Allie married Wade strictly for his money?

CHAPTER SIX

Wade watched his horse prance with the knowledge that they were about to go for a ride. He laughed and led the big bay out into the sunshine.

"Hold on, Bay Boy. You're going to get your chance in just a second, after I make a stop at the kitchen."

He had to tell Allie where he was going and make sure she was okay. He'd spotted her standing on the patio when he'd looked toward the house earlier. Even in the distance, her blonde hair glistened in the sun and he could see her almost too slim figure. Grief. Stress. Worry. All emotions she'd been overwhelmed with could make a person lose their appetite and he wondered whether this was why she was so thin. She was so worried about her mom and still hurting at the sudden death of her father, and then the financial strain on her all could have made her look so fragile. The strength of his need to protect her startled him. And then there was the lightning strike.

A few years ago, he'd been very near the spot that lightning had struck a tree. The electrical force that radiated from the strike caused a sizzle to race through him and the hair on the back of his neck to stand up. This was the feeling he'd experienced earlier when he'd felt eyes on him and had looked toward the house and saw Allie standing in the morning sunlight.

He hadn't been able to move at first. He'd just stared as the hum of electrical energy sizzled through him. And then he'd lifted his hand and tipped his hat.

He was too far away to clearly see her eyes but they were locked on him; he could feel it. And he'd seen them in his memory: large, half trusting, half wary. And when she'd lifted her own hand to wave, he'd felt the sparks all the way to his toes.

He was fighting to ignore the attraction. Knew all too well that all women were not as they seemed. He wanted to believe Allie was exactly what she appeared but he'd been burned so many times that this was hard to shake.

And then there was the fact that he loved his granddaddy but Wade had no plans to let anyone dictate how he lived his life. Not even Granddaddy.

"You're in control when it comes to your lady friends, Bay Boy," he said softly as the horse nudged him and gave him a dark-eyed stare. "I'm taking pointers from you. Never letting a woman have control over my happiness." *He was talking to his horse about his new wife.* And as if he had conjured her up, she suddenly appeared around the corner of the barn, looking fresh and pretty and causing his heart to stumble when those eyes of hers connected with his.

He cinched up his runaway libido, yanked it hard to get his focus back on not letting her get to him. She was beautiful and those eyes just seemed to dig in to his heart. No, not his heart—his…mind. There were twelve inches between his brain and his heart and it was his brain that she was affecting.

He had never, ever had the kind of reaction to a woman that he had with Allie and he was just getting his boots back under him. That was all. But it wasn't her fault she was having this strange effect on him, so he smiled and willed himself to act normal. She here and they had an agreement and he needed to treat her kindly, despite the need to get tough with himself.

"Good morning, sunshine. I see you were up and about early. I guess you got everything figured out and back into my room? It's a good view from up there, isn't it?"

"The view is beautiful. It's amazing. You have the Guadalupe right in your backyard. That's just cool."

"No, it's actually the Pedernales River."

"Oh, you can tell I haven't been around here that much."

"There are a lot of rivers in the region but the Guadalupe is the best known."

"Well, the important thing is that your grandfather

picked well. It's just beautiful here. Breathtaking. I can see why you love it so much."

He stared at her with her twinkling eyes and excitement. He loved this land and liked that she saw it for what it was and liked it. And not for the fact that it was sitting on a lot of black oil, or as his granddaddy called it black gold.

"Texas is a smorgasbord of terrain spread across all five regions. This area is like a slice of them all. Did you sleep well?"Her gaze shifted to him. "As well as I could, with the different aspects of what I've committed to with you hammering at me. My brain didn't want to shut down but at some point during the night I drifted off. I met Nelda and she's lovely. I'm so not used to being waited on."

"She won't push you. I don't want it either but I do like not having to cook. That's why she puts everything in the fridge or leaves it on the stove for me to get for myself."

"What are you doing?" She looked from him to his horse.

She was nervous. He understood the feeling. She

was also shifting the conversation away from her lack of sleep. He could see the faint purple under her eyes and knew she wasn't sleeping, whether she told him about it or didn't.

"You look like you are going riding," she said, when he didn't answer her question.

"Right. I've been gone for almost a week, so I need to ride out and check on some of the cowboys while they're working cattle today. I normally would do it on a four-wheeler, or just go in the truck but I've been out of the saddle for several days and both me and Bay Boy need the exercise. I'm riding to a little fence over in the north pasture that was repaired by a company that we hired and I want to take a look at it and see if I'll hire them to do any more work. I don't want them to do it if it's not going to be a good job. What are you going to do? Would you want to come?" The question came out before he realized he was going to ask it.

"Well, um, I hate to say it but I've lived in Texas my whole life and I don't know a lot about cows and ranch life. Now, Ginny does. She knows the difference between a cow and bull." She laughed, looking embarrassed.

She was cute. "Surely you know that?"

She turned pink. "Well, that's the big joke. I think I've got it straightened out now."

He wasn't sure whether she was joking or not and he was afraid to laugh—but when she made a cute scrunched face and laughed, his own laughter won out.

They stared at each other, a feeling of comradery settling between them for that moment. It felt nice.

Finally, he said, "Bulls have equipment that cows don't have and cows have equipment that bulls don't have. It's a pretty major distinction. And visible. You were joking, right?"

She turned the color of a ripe strawberry. He hated he'd embarrassed her but on a ranch, there was a lot of breeding going on so it was a common subject.

"Well, not completely serious," she hedged. "But in a way...at one point I didn't realize that cows could have horns. Ginny set me straight and told me that was one piece of equipment either female or male can have and I didn't realize that."

That sizzle raced between them and he stamped it out and concentrated on the conversation. "Well, Ginny would be right about that. So, what's her story?" he asked, curious about the woman who was Allie's friend and so different than her.

"She was raised on a vineyard. They had a few head of cattle, which she says justifies her love of cowgirl hats. She's got a collection. She's always trying to get me to wear one of them but I feel awkward in a hat and never do. Kind of squashes my face down and it's not a good look. And, well, a girl has got to do what she can."

He thought she would look good in anything she put on her head but he didn't tell her that. This girl and Ginny were two very different people. It was hard to put them as best friends.

"What about that ride? You never answered me."

"You're really, seriously inviting me to go riding?" she asked with a look of complete disbelief on her pretty face. "You need to work and I might get in the way."

His gut tightened and he realized that he really

wanted her to go along with him.

"Yeah, I do. You're going to be here for three months and like you said, you're going to get bored and you'll want to do something. So the best thing is to jump in there and let me show you the place. So maybe somewhere along the way you'll see something that hits a chord in you and might interest you to do."

"I'm not going to repair a fence."

He laughed. "Funny. We'll find you something. Lord knows I would get bored out of my mind if I was just sittin' around. I'd probably go stir-crazy."

Her lips twitched. "Something told me that's how you felt. I bet you work from morning until night."

"And love every minute of it."

"I thought so." She raked a hand through her thick hair and looked at Bay Boy weirdly. "You're going to give me one that's not likely going to bolt? I have visions of me on the back of a horse flying across the pastures, barely hanging on as you race behind me, trying to catch up so you can save me before we reach the cliffs."

He stared at her, his mind envisioning what she

had just said. "You have been watching way too many movies."

She laughed. "Hey, they all have that in them, or some variation of it. You promise me that's not going to happen to me? I mean, the Guadalupe is out there— oh, sorry, the Pedernales is out there. And some cliffs."

He shook his head and grinned at her. Something he was doing a lot since marrying her. "I promise you that those cliffs you're seeing I do own but we won't be crossing the river. I'm not taking any chances in making that vision of yours come true. Even as far-fetched as that would be for Ladybug, the horse you will be riding, to do. I don't even think she would do that if she got a bee up under her saddle. How's that sound?"

"Well, it actually sounds romantic. You know, like the old Westerns where he rescues the damsel from the runaway horse or the stagecoach heading for destruction."

She was funny. "You have one major imagination."

"I know. I've always been a book lover. Growing

up, I planted my nose in a book as often as possible."

"Sounds like you should write your own stories."

She laughed disbelievingly. "Oh no, I would never be able to write. I can't spell well and I was a terrible English student. Writing wouldn't be for me."

"I think you should give it a shot. I'm going to saddle Ladybug for you. She hasn't been ridden in a while, so you're going to make her day."

He went to the fence and whistled, glancing back to see Allie's smile as she watched the small horse come trotting toward them. When he saw the smile of delight on Allie's face, satisfaction swarmed through him. It was going to be a good day. As hard as it had been for him to believe that was possible after being forced to marry a total stranger, at the moment none of that mattered. Destressing Allie and seeing delight on her face made it all seem, for now, worth it all.

She was going horseback riding with Wade. Her husband. *Her hunky, gorgeous, cowboy husband.* As she'd been standing there talking with him, she had felt drawn to him in so many ways.

She eyed the adorable, multicolored horse with the sweet face and eyes that were so calming that Allie had no fear. "So, what do I do to get on this horse? Ladybug looks exactly like the kind of horse I would get along with fantastically."

"I think so too, that's why I'm saddling her for you."

"Wade, thank you. I'm really looking forward to this. The last few months have been so awful with the wreck, my poor dad's death and then my mom…I've been under so much pressure I haven't really had a chance to grieve my dad. And as I was walking across the parking lot out here and listening to the birds singing and seeing this beautiful place, I've just had this huge weight lifted off my shoulders." Her voice wobbled. "Wade, I just feel happy right now."

She had been tied up in knots with worry and grief and some depression because she was failing her daddy when she couldn't take care of her mama. It was just the worst feeling in the world. Thinking about it, her tears welled in her eyes and she swiped them away really quick and gave a short laugh. "I didn't mean to start crying. I mean, I'm happy and I'm grateful. And I just need to tell you that again."

Wade moved to her side and wrapped his arms around her, pulling her close. She laid her head on his chest and felt his wonderful heart beating against her temple and his strong arms holding her protectively against him. She felt comfort she hadn't known since the wreck that had changed her life. His hand gently rubbed the tense muscles between her shoulder blades.

"It's okay, Allie. I totally understand. And I'm so glad when I was in that truck stop you asked about how I was doing. Because I couldn't bring myself to ask anyone else. I was out of options. I'm so grateful to you, too. And I promise you I'm going to do everything I can to help you. So that when you walk away from this in three months, you'll be as happy and maybe a little more worry-free than you are right now. I'm so sorry about your daddy. I understand grief…I'm still grieving my grandpa. Man, I loved that man. He was taken too soon. And I know your daddy was taken too soon. And I'm praying for your mama. Is she going to be okay?"

She sighed. "I'm not sure she will recover. But thanks to you and the Lord bringing you into that truck stop when He did, I'm giving Mama her best shot."

Getting all the courage she could muster, she lifted her head from his shoulder and looked up at him, which was kinda bad because that put her face really close to his jaw and his lips. He looked at her with those gorgeous eyes and all she could think about was that kiss yesterday when they had been pronounced man and wife. Her knees went weak and she knew she needed to move. "I hope you and your brothers find peace with your granddaddy's death and the will. It is such a blessing to me…I can't help but believe he meant it for good in some way."

She took a deep breath and willed herself to stop looking at his lips. She forced herself to say what she needed to say. "Maybe this is his way to get you to test the waters of marriage. And then later you'll fall in love the right way. I mean, you'll really fall in love and you'll get married and you'll fill this place with babies and he'll look down from heaven with a big smile on his face."

"Maybe." His gaze sought hers out. "But I'm not planning on marrying for real."

To her surprise, he kissed her forehead. It was gentle and warm and sent thrills of tingling sensations shooting throughout her entire body.

As if realizing what he'd done, he released her. "You're a very positive person. But in all honesty, it would take a miracle for me to really marry. And I think Granddaddy knew that. This is his last-ditch effort to try to change my resolve. It's not happening. Let's ride."

She backed a few steps away from him, tempted to embarrass herself by throwing her arms around him and planting her lips against his. That would only embarrass them both. "Get me on that horse and let's do this. How's that for positive thinking?"

CHAPTER SEVEN

It was a beautiful May morning, warming up but not too warm to keep them from enjoying the ride. And the wildflowers were still blooming before the July heat came in and burned everything up. It was a good time for her to be here. By the end of July, it would be really hot and it wouldn't be so enjoyable for her.

They rode slowly through several pastures, with him paying special attention to helping her be comfortable in the saddle. In between instructions, they talked about the different wildflowers as they rode. When they rode over the crest and he saw Clay and several of his other ranch hands, Allie gasped.

"It looks just like a scene from a movie, with them branding them and whatever else they're doing."

It did look that way, he realized. "They're giving them shots against certain illnesses and things like that."

"Oh, I don't want to brand a cow."

He grinned. "I didn't think you did."

In the end, she watched. And then let him know as they were riding away after saying good-bye to the other cowboys, that that was not something she wanted to spend her time doing while she was here for three months.

"I assumed as much." He'd laughed. "But I have something in mind."

After watching the men work cattle, they rode to the river.

Allie stared at the rushing water and the wide expanse of the river. "I'm still in awe about how beautiful this place is. Do you ever float down this river—you know, like they do on the Guadalupe?"

"Not much. But you'll find people who do. Not like they do in New Braunfels. Or in Hunt, Texas. You know, the Guadalupe starts up there near Hunt. You can walk right there to the very end of it, see it coming up out of the sandstone."

She stared at him. "You actually can see where the river starts?"

"Yeah, it's pretty cool. I haven't been down there in a while but there's a real cute little resort. It's nothing fancy. We used to go there when I was a kid. You can canoe from right there to the end of it and park your canoe and wade right up to the end of it. It's really cool. I mean, there are spots in it that the water has hollowed out the sandstone and you can sit in it like a bathtub or something and let the water pool around you. And if you keep walking up, you get to where you're just wading through real thin water and you can actually see it bubbling up out of the ground."

"Wow. That would be interesting to see."

"Maybe we can go before you leave and I can show you."

"I would like that, if you end up having the time."

"We'll do it. I'll call them and book the room for a night. We'll go up there and we'll do that."

This man could really be right up there with the best person she'd ever met in her entire life. She was still having a hard time realizing he was worth as much money as he was worth. Talking to him, you'd never know it. And she kept forgetting about it all day until she would spot one of the black steel oil pumping stations.

She got off Ladybug and tied the reins to a tree branch. "I want to put my toes in it. Is that okay?" He got off the horse, too, and tied him to the tree branch beside Ladybug. "I'll watch you put your toes in. I'm not going to take my boots off."

She hurried over to a big flat rock beside the water. She bent down and untied her tennis shoes, and set them on a rock. She stood and he stepped beside her as she walked to the river and stuck her toe in the water.

Instantly, she jumped. "Oh my gosh! It's cold! It's like ice water."

"Yup, it's quite a jolt."

She stuck her hand in the water and felt the coolness of it and let her fingers drift through the water as she looked at it. "I'm not sure I could get in that but it is really lovely. I love watching water rush by like that. Does it ever get out of the banks down here—I mean, like with the flash floods and you know, when we have the rains and everything?"

He sobered. "Yeah. You'll have to be careful and heed flash flood warnings. It can be dangerous."

"Okay, I will." Her stomach growled. She had only eaten that bacon this morning but she wasn't going to tell him that. She was definitely going to be ready to eat when they got back to the house. But this had been a remarkable day and she had loved every moment of it. On the way back, after riding by the fence he had wanted to check out, they passed a small barn not too far from view of the house. "What's that?"

"I'll show that to you on another day. I'm gonna get you home right now so you can eat. But that's where we keep the calves whose mothers didn't have milk or for some reason abandoned them. We bottle feed them."

"Really? I'd love to see that. I mean, I'd like to try to feed a calf. I've never fed a calf before."

"Well then, tomorrow or the next day, we'll come down here and I'll let you feed one. However, I really have to get back for a conference call this afternoon. I'll show you the foals too."

"Sounds wonderful." And it truly did.

By the time the evening had come around, Allie had explored the grounds around the house and she'd even considered taking a swim in the pool. But she decided against it for now. It was going to take some getting used to being here at this beautiful place. She had ended up on the side terrace that was made of tile and bordered with a sandstone rock foot high ledge. She had a view of the barn and stable.

She could get used to ranch life. It was busy and alive and there was so much going on. She'd watched cowboys ride in on horseback and dismount and head into the barns and stables. She'd also watched other cowboys drive in, pulling trailer loads of cattle. And there had been others ride up over the horizon on four-wheel all-terrain vehicles.

Wade had said they used those, too, and she thought it would be fun. She had enjoyed spending time with him and getting to know him. Now, he was in his office working on paperwork, she assumed, and she continued to sit out on the terrace outside of the kitchen and large family room. It had a very similar view as the one from his bedroom but from a different angle and more a view of a wider swath of river. But it was a good distance from the house and there were a lot more cattle between her and the river. The sun was starting to set lower in the sky and as she sat there, it truly occurred to her that about now, she would've been going to work at the truck stop and she would've just left checking on her mom at the rehabilitation center. She felt a pang of guilt at not being there. She would call again tomorrow and make sure everything was still going well there. She had been reassured several times that there was really no reason for her to come to the center every day. Still, it was hard not to want to be there to make sure everything was okay.

She closed her eyes and tried to let the peace of the evening fill her as she rocked in the rustic porch swing. The barns had quieted down; the cowboys had gone for the day. She rocked in the swing and just sat there. Until now, she had very little time to just sit and think and she wasn't sure what to do with herself. But for a moment, she was indulgent and she didn't move or let her mind roam to her responsibilities.

The door behind her opened and she turned to see Wade step out onto the veranda. As usual, her heart did a little skip when she saw him and butterflies danced in her stomach and rose into her chest. He smiled an easy smile and every cell in her body just went crazy.

"You enjoying the evening? Mind if I join you?"

She patted the swing she was sitting in. "It is lovely. It's so nice out. I was just enjoying watching the cowboys finish up for the day then hurry home. And then letting the peace of the evening settle in around me. I'm still trying to adjust to the fact that I'm actually here. I know, I know…I'm like a broken record."

"No, I'm totally getting where you're coming from. Today was nice." He sat down in the swing and it creaked with his weight.

She was very aware of the fact that there was only about twelve inches between them on the seat. He placed both hands on his thighs and rubbed them very slowly to his knees and back, as if he were nervous. That was almost laughable. He didn't seem to be the nervous type to her. But she was. She clasped her hands together in her lap and yes, her palms were slightly damp. Not very ladylike but that's just the way it was at the moment. The man made her nervous. Like, really nervous. He'd showered at some point and smelled of spicy soap and light aftershave...or probably some expensive cologne. She inhaled deeply, enjoying the scent.

"Nelda left some lasagna in the oven warming for us." He rested an arm along the back of the swing. "And some garlic bread. Whenever you feel like you're hungry, we can eat, inside or, if you prefer, out here on the veranda as my grandmother always called it."

She smiled at him. "Out here, please. And it's so large, I actually thought of it as a veranda myself."

"Growing up, we had all our family gatherings out here, including my Granddaddy's brother and all of his family. He had one son, Uncle Jude, who had four kids. We were all around the same age and a rowdy bunch, It was nice though. We would barbecue and swim in the pool. It was much louder than it is now. I can tell you, a herd of little boys and one very hard headed girl are not quiet. I remember back then my granddaddy was really happy. He was preoccupied with work, as always because he was building up the ranch. By then, he'd hit oil and instead of sitting back and enjoying the royalties, he'd started expanding. He'd been successful before the oil and had dreams, but the oil multiplied his dreams."

"It sounds like you had a great family life at that point. I'm sorry about your parents. Did they die young?"

"Yeah. Dad was about thirty-two, Morgan's age. And Mom was barely thirty. Dad had a private plane license and had gotten a new plane. Granddaddy had a pilot who usually flew them on longer trips but he got sick the night they were supposed to go to Las Vegas for the National Finals Rodeo. Dad decided to fly them and a storm blew in and the plane went down. Everybody on board was lost, including Uncle Jude and his wife, Tina. That left my four second cousins without parents too. Great Uncle Talbert raised them down the road on his ranch. You'll meet them soon."

Allie's heart clutched. "I'm so sorry. What a huge loss for your whole family."

He turned slightly to look at her; his head was tilted and there was sympathy in his gaze. "You understand completely. I mean, you lost your dad. It's hard. Grief knots you up inside. But eventually you have to move forward."

She took a shuddering breath, emotions suddenly hitting her in a wave. "Yes. Nobody really understands except those who have lived it."

He nodded and glanced down at the pastures, lost in thought momentarily. She didn't even know whether he realized that his fingers had gathered up a strand of her hair and were toying with it. It felt as though he wasn't even aware that he was doing it. She, however, was very aware of it.

How long had it been since she'd felt this level of awareness? This level of companionship? She had Ginny but that was different on so many levels.

"It seems very lonesome for you now." She glanced at him.

He didn't turn his head back to her but he let his gaze slide to hers for a brief touch before he nodded and looked back at the pastures. "Yeah, it is, I miss Granddaddy something fierce but I have my work. And my brothers. And my cousins too. Everyone is busy but we know we're there for each other. Like you and your friend Ginny are there for each other. Being lonesome...it's not something I think about too much. Well, sometimes, but there are a whole lot of things far worse than being lonesome."

What does that mean? She wanted to ask him but it was very intrusive. She bit her lip and enjoyed the feel of his fingers toying with her hair. Thought about that kiss. And despite everything in her telling her to stop thinking about it, she did. She thought about his arms going around her right now and pulling her close and kissing her right there on that swing on his grandmother's veranda. And then her mind went crazy with the fantasy that they were really in love and really were married in the true sense of the word. And she really was a part of this…and she was going to spend the rest of her life here with him, sharing this incredible life with babies and that she would live happily ever after with the man of her dreams.

She stiffened. *What was she thinking?*

"Something wrong?"

She looked at him and she knew that she probably looked guilty. *If he could read her thoughts, what would he say?* She swallowed hard. "N-no."

He stared at her and she didn't think it was her imagination that it suddenly got hotter sitting there. Like the breeze that had been blowing dried up and somebody turned on an industrial-sized blow-dryer.

"Do you know you have the most beautiful blue eyes I have ever seen? And they're really big. It's almost like I can see my reflection in them. Or a pool of cool water." He smiled and tugged ever so slightly on the strand of hair.

Oh dear, what was she supposed to say to that? Her heart galloped. "Yeah, I've always been told my eyes were huge. When I was a kid, they were almost the biggest thing about me. I've always been small."

"You're small but are you normally this thin? I'm a little worried about you."

He was worried about her? The statement did funny things to her entire system. *When was the last time anyone had told her they were worried about her?*

"Thank you for worrying but I'm okay. And I've been eating. I've lost about ten pounds since my daddy died. I needed to lose five, but not that way. I just don't have that big an appetite. And then, you know, I worry about my mom and then working at the truck stop when it was a busy night, I did a lot of walking. But you've swept me away from all of that to this life of leisure." She teased him to ease the sudden emotions swirling inside her. This man stirred things inside her she was scared to get too close to.

He laughed huskily. "You deserve it and hopefully will take advantage of it while you can. Speaking of eating, let's put some food in you and see if we can help you gain that ten pounds back."

She hadn't missed the "while you can" phrase. A reminder that she was not staying here. She wasn't sure he caught that he'd said it but she had. And she would do well to remember that this was not her home. She was simply passing through for a brief moment in time.

CHAPTER EIGHT

Wade drove over to the vineyard first thing the next morning to tell Todd he'd married. He'd called Morgan, who was at the resort headquarters in Houston, and his oldest brother had not been happy. Not about what Granddaddy had done and not that Wade had had to jump through hoops to get it done. As Wade walked past the house—or villa, as they called the huge home that housed Todd's living quarters and the tasting room and event venue—and headed toward the fields of grapes where Todd had told him he would be when he'd texted him earlier, he replayed Morgan's words.

"He's pulling our chains and I still haven't forgiven him for it. I know he's going to force my hand with the hotels just like he's doing with you. And probably going to do the same with Todd. I still haven't decided what I'm going to do when my time comes."

"Look, Morgan, you know good and well that you'll do what you need to do. I don't care one way or the other. I saved the ranch and that's what matters to me. Allie will get what she needs and at the end of this, we will walk away. Done deal. You can do that too. But, don't judge me. I can hear it in your voice."

"I'm not judging you. I'm just wary. If you're lucky, everything will work out like you hope. But what if it doesn't? What if she figures out a way to get her hooks into you?"

"She's a nice person and you know how judgmental I am of women and their motives."

"We'll see, brother. We'll see. Good luck."

"Come meet her." Wade threw the invite out there. *Why did Morgan need to meet Allie?* She wasn't going to be around after three months.

They'd ended the call knowing they had differing views. But since when was that new between brothers? Now to tell Todd.

He found him looking frustrated in a patch of grapes they were planting.

"You don't look happy."

"You wouldn't be either, if you'd just lost your master winemaker you'd be frowning too."

"No kidding?"

"Yeah, just took an offer in Italy he couldn't pass up."

Wade was stunned but knew his brother would land on his feet. "I'd say leaving you was a pretty wrong move on his part. You have an excuse to find a better one now."

Todd shot him a yeah-right glare. "Postive thinkin' is good, I'm just not there at the moment."

Wade grinned. "You will be. Though I know it's hard on you thinking about having to do more than walk through your fields, enjoying your grapes?"

Todd's frown deepened. "Right, that's all I do

around here."

Wade always enjoyed annoying his younger brother. "You didn't plant those—your help did. And the master winemaker did everything else."

"Right. You're real funny."

Wade chuckled. "You know I'm aggravating you on purpose."

"I know, and I took your bait."

"You always do."

"Not true. I'm just feeling edgy. All this stuff with Granddaddy is still needling at me. You're about to lose the ranch and then it'll be my turn or Morgan's. I hope granddaddy is happy." He paused, then stared at him. Wade grinned at him. He frowned more, if that were possible. "Today is the last day of the deal. Why are you grinning, what are you going to do now?"

He was right. This would have been the day he'd have lost the ranch if it wasn't for Allie marrying him. Gratefulness washed over him and his grin widened as relief so strong slammed into him and a short laugh of release escaped him.

"Why are you laughing?" Todd's eyes narrowed.

"Because, I had forgotten today was the day and that's what I came to tell you. I'm married. I saved the ranch."

"What? When?" Todd looked at him in disbelief and shock.

"Three days ago. Found her at a truck stop. That sounds wrong. I went into the truck stop and was probably looking like a hound dog that had lost its mate. I was just sitting there, drinking coffee, lost in thought, and she was working herself into the ground waiting on the tables all by herself. But she still kept coming by, worrying over me, refilling my coffee and asking me if I wanted something to eat. Finally, she just ordered pancakes for me. And when she brought them over, the place had calmed down and she asked me if everything was all right. She was sincere. And I told her. Turns out she was also in need and desperate to help her mother. We came to a mutually beneficial agreement and got married."

Todd looked incredulous. "You really went through with it?"

"I did. And I wanted to come tell you. In three

months, the ranch will be ours again—without strings attached."

"I can't believe it." He took a deep breath and stared out at the vines. "I don't know what I'll do if he puts the same stipulations on me and this place."

"You're a stubborn, hard-nosed, determined cowboy. You'll take care of business."

Todd cocked his head. "I like to think so, but marrying someone…I'm not so sure."

Wade laughed, still feeling relief. "You'll do it. If that's what Granddaddy drops on you. It's going to be interesting."

Todd's lip twitched. "What are you talking about? You still have three months to make it to the finish line. I figure that's going to be interesting, and harder than you think to make work."

"Nope, Allie's nice. It's like I told Morgan. She's nice and will walk away. Nothing's going to go wrong."

"I hope not."

Todd's last words followed Wade back to his truck. *Did he have something to worry about like both his brothers seemed to think?*

They didn't know Allie. There wasn't going to be a problem. Not on her part and not on his part. Everything was good. Heck, everything was great. The ranch was his again.

Three days after arriving at the ranch, Allie stood beside Wade and stared at the four calves inside the pen.

"Now, I'm warning you," Wade drawled slowly, squinting at her from beneath his straw hat. She looked from him to the calves looking at her from the other side of the fence. "They might look sweet and they're not that big. However, looks can be deceiving because these little mischievous devils are *very* rambunctious. And you being small and not weighing a whole heck of a lot are going to make them think they have a new toy."

She laughed, feeling uncertain. "You are joking, right?"

"Hardly. When they go to jerking on those bottles,

you'll see. I'm just hoping I don't see you facedown in the muck, being dragged around like a stuffed doll. If it happens, let go."

She laughed incredulously. "You are kidding. They're only three feet tall."

"With the muscle of a hundred and fifty pound man." He hitched both brows at her in a cocky mark-my-word expression.

He looked cute in that moment but she didn't dare tell him that. "Whatever. But really, it can't be that hard." She'd do this just to show him she wasn't the wimp he obviously thought she was.

"We'll give it a try. But until you get some more meat on those bones, they might be hard to handle. They're like goats—they'll come up and butt, so be ready or next thing you know, you'll be getting butted from the other side and you'll be in that dirt smelling like all that nice stuff that they leave on the ground over there. Get my drift?"

She laughed. The guy got to her. "Believe me, you are coming across loud and clear. I get what you're saying. I will try to stay off the ground. Now show me how to do this."

He'd brought four large bottles with him that looked as if they were about twelve to fifteen inches tall, with huge red nipples on the end of them. She watched with interest as he opened the gate and scooted inside, then distracted the rambunctious crew and motioned for her to follow him.

She slid through the small crack then hooked the chain over the nail head like she'd seen him undo a moment ago.

"Stay right by me." He set two bottles on the top of a pole that was about twelve inches around, with the top sawed off. It made the perfect shelf—up high enough that the calves couldn't reach the bottles. Then he handed her one of the bottles and he kept one in his hand.

She looked at the bottle. "All right, I'm going to do whatever you show me but goodness, will they drink all this?"

"In a heartbeat. After they slobber all over you. It's not the greatest job in the world but newbies seem to like it, so this might be just the job for you."

"I'm not so enthusiastic about the slobbering part."

He laughed. "Comes with the territory."

He held the bottle out and the calves about broke their necks clamoring over one another to see who got the red nipple first. They were surrounded by the mooing black calves, their big saggy ears dangling as they jostled. The long-limbed sweeties were adorable. One of them latched onto the nipple then kicked the other one in the ribs and Allie cringed.

"Ouch, that had to hurt." She decided she'd better plan for some defensive moves herself or she'd have some sore ribs.

He laughed. "See what I'm talking about? Now hold yours out there and I'm telling you to hold on to the bottle tightly or you're going to lose it. But you better set your feet apart for balance."

She did as she was told, feeling as if she were about to join the NFL or something.

"Good. Now get ready because you don't want to lose your balance when they latch on."

She saw how aggressive the calf was yanking on

his bottle and was prepared. "I just cannot even imagine it would be this way." She posed the bottle out there in front of her very carefully, wary of what was about to happen. But excited too. Instantly, the calves jumped at the bottle. One of them latched on and yanked so hard Allie had to take two steps forward. But she held on. However, she started to laugh. She could not help it. The harder the calf pulled, the harder she laughed.

"Hey, get a handle on yourself," Wade drawled. Then, when she couldn't stop, he laughed too.

She was going to be dragged all over the place if she didn't get control of her senses. But it was so funny. Suddenly, one of the calves that did not get to the bottle in time threw itself at her. The hard knock sent her stumbling sideways and straight into Wade's side. It was like hitting a brick wall. His free arm slid around her in an instant and he held her plastered to his side, or she would have fallen at his feet. She'd managed to hang onto the bottle; the calf managed to hang onto the nipple and her free hand grabbed hold of Wade's waistband, the leather belt giving her fingers something to latch onto. Which was good as her gaze locked with Wade's.

"Whoa there," he said softly, a startled smile on his face as their gazes held. "You okay?"

Her heart banged away inside her like a sledgehammer and her knees had turned to water but he was holding her up, so she was still standing. "Sure," she croaked. "Thanks for catching me."

"Any time." His eyes warmed and she felt his heart thundering against hers.

Wade smiled. "I never had anyone start laughing like that before."

"I couldn't help it. I do that sometimes. If something gets me tickled, I can't always stop."

"Fine by me. It's probably been the most enjoyable time I've ever had feeding these critters."

"Glad to be entertaining." She tried to straighten up. Either that or she'd combust right there in his arms.

He held her arm after she'd moved away from the protection of his body and the circle of his arm. She wanted to dive right back in there but refrained.

"Now, ready for the new trick?"

"I think so."

"I'm going to hang on to this bottle with one hand, and see how I'm snugging it up against my hip? It's to help me hold on. Now I'm going to reach up here." He smiled and took a bottle from the post. "You're going to have to do what I'm doing and balance that bottle against your hip like that and kinda lock that hand around it so you have a good grip on it."

She did as he asked and then he handed her the other bottle.

Their fingers touched and she had no time to think about the energy that zipped up her arm at just the mere graze of his skin against hers.

"Good...you got it. Now balance that one against your hip and hang on because that other calf is going to come get it. I'm going to do it to the other one and won't have an arm to rescue you with, while we feed two at a time." He reached up and grabbed the other bottle and propped it against his hip and held on with his other hand. Immediately, the other two calves latched on to their bottle tips and started nursing.

She could do this. She did the same and held on.

Instantly, she was being yanked from side to side but they kind of balanced each other out. This was definitely an aggressive endeavor.

"I feel like I'm playing contact sports or something."

"Yeah, it can feel that way. But you're doing great."

She *was* doing great, she decided after a few minutes. She was proud she hadn't dirt dived. Then the bottle of the first calf suddenly came up empty. And he did not like that at all. He latched his teeth onto that nipple, set his hooves in the dirt and yanked violently, setting her off-balance as he started backing up then suddenly let go and bolted toward her. She stumbled back just as the other calf yanked on the other bottle. The next thing she knew, she fell back into the dirt and something warm and damp—and smelly—spread out beneath her back.

"Allie, are you okay?" Wade jumped between her and the calves, dropping his bottles as he held his hands out to her.

She swallowed hard and tried not to think about

what she was laying in. "I'm fine. Oh gosh, I stink," she squeaked, feeling squeamish.

He laughed. "Sorry. It happens. Here, take my hands and let's get you out of here and cleaned up."

She looked up at him with his contagious smile. Her heart lifted and she smiled back at him, not caring hardly at all that her back was wet and she stunk. She slipped her hands into his and let him tug her to her feet. One of the calves broke past Wade and head-butted her in the hip. She yelped and suddenly found herself scooped up into Wade's arms.

"Oh." She gasped. "What are you doing?"

He smiled. "I'm rescuing you."

"But I stink and I'm getting that—that nasty muck on my back on you."

"I'm a cowboy. I work in muck half the time. Besides, I missed saving you from falling into it. I deserve to suffer just like you. Are you okay?"

She was floored by his attitude. "I'm fine. But I still feel bad for you. I'm *really* icky."

He stopped at the gate and his gaze swept over her face. "You're really lovely."

"No," she denied.

His eyes drilled into her. "Yes. Really."

Allie's throat went dry. "Okay, but I'm dying here from the fumes engulfing me."

"Okay, your wish is my command. If you'll unhook the chain, I'll sweep you out of here and dump you in a trough somewhere."

She reached for the chain and was laughing as he carried her through the gate, then waited for her to hook the chain back. He grinned at her then continued to carry her even though the calves were not slamming into her any longer. Her hands had somehow wrapped around his neck and she wasn't sure she would let go when he got her to wherever he was taking her.

"Where is this trough my knight in cowboy boots and Stetson is taking me to get cleaned up?" she asked, trying to keep the sudden longing she was feeling hidden beneath a lighthearted tone.

"Right over there. But I'm not tossing you into a trough. A simple water hose will do."

She saw where he pointed. A water hose was hooked up to a water line at the end of the small barn.

Her hands tightened around him and she realized she was wishing he would walk really slow so she could continue to enjoy the feeling of being in his arms, of being held between them and his hard chest.

When they reached the faucet, all too soon, he gently set her on her feet and she reluctantly let go of him…and fought hard to not look as if she were struggling. "I see that. I had no idea all this was involved in feeding those cute little fellas out there." She turned the nozzle on and handed him the water hose. "Spray me down, please."

He laughed. "Of course you didn't. And I would be glad to spray you down, and me too. We both stink to high heaven."

She gaped at him. "You said you were used to it."

"I am, but we still smell terrible. Not to mention we are pretty gross."

"I agree. Now spray, please."

She didn't have to ask again; he pulled the trigger on the nozzle at the end of the hose and blasted her back with a heavy stream of water. She giggled and then, unable to help herself, she surprised him by grabbing the nozzle from his hands and shooting him down with a stream of water.

"Hey, that wasn't fair." He laughed and then tried to take it back. She dodged him and then hooted with laughter as he grabbed her hands and the water sprayed him in the face, knocking his hat off and soaking his hair. "That is so not fair," he said, his words garbled as the water got him momentarily in the mouth.

She dropped the hose then, overcome with laughter. "I know, right? But oh, it was so fun."

They stood there, smiling and laughing and dripping, as they stared at each other.

He lifted a hand and pushed some hair from her face. Water streamed down her chin. "I think maybe we better find you another job."

She gasped. "Hey, buster, I think not. I'm doing this job. I'm not a quitter. I'll get better at it. I mean, really, I can't get worse, so things are already looking up."

"You have a point. And you'll get it figured out." He grinned at her. "So, I have to go into town later this afternoon. I'm going to have to pick up some supplies. Want to ride into town with me?"

"Yes." She was going to enjoy going to see the little town and well, she was going to have to fit in for three months, so there was no better time to check everything out than right now. "I want to. I guess I can change before we go?" She was soaking wet and still stunk. She might be rinsed off but she was far from clean.

"I think that would be really good. Who knows—I may change too."

They laughed and headed toward the truck, detouring so he could go back into the pen to grab the bottles from the ground where the calves were still trying to get milk from them and having little luck.

She laughed when he held the dented bottles up. "They pretty much did these in."

"I'm so sorry I lost hold of them."

"Not a problem. I have plenty where these came from," he said, as he came back to the fence, tossed the bottles outside the fence then had to shoo the calves back before coming back out of the gate and locking it behind him.

When they reached the truck Allie stopped. "Oh no, we're going to mess up the inside of your truck."

"It'll clean up."

"But I'm soaked. And that crud that still lingers on my back is far from sanitary."

"You're fine. This is my work truck. Believe me, ranch work gets messy. If I was always worrying about my truck, then I wouldn't get any work done."

She conceded with a sigh. This wasn't the truck he'd been driving when he drove into the truck stop and brought her here in after the wedding. That truck had been top of the line. This one was plain, with the McCoy's Rocking M Ranch logo on the side. "Okay, if you say so."

"I say so. Now, up you go." He'd opened the door and now held her elbow as she stepped up on the running board and then sat on the edge of the seat. "You can lean back."

"I know. I'm having to ease into it."

His lips twitched and he laid a hand on her knee, which warmed her damp skin instantly. "You are not going to hurt the seat."

And then he stepped back and closed the door. She watched him as she sat there with her hand on her knee where his hand had been, feeling the warm tingle of awareness that remained where he'd touched her.

CHAPTER NINE

The town was cute. It was the usual rustic Texas town with a square that looked like if given a chance could die. The reality was there wasn't a whole lot there. Dixie's Diner was a little building at the end of a sidewalk with more empty old buildings than filled. There were a couple of antiques stores and trucks that told the story of ranching communities.

"Stonewall isn't a big place. We have Fredericksburg on one side of us, a powerhouse of shopping and tourism, and then we have Johnson City on the other end. It's a tourist attraction, too, and a great place. So we get people passing through but our businesses struggle and come and go. There's a lot going on around Stonewall, with all the ranches, and peach farms and wineries. And of course, the presidential state park. But none of it is enough to help us compete. Dixie's hangs in there, though, and caters to cowboys wanting home-cooked food and great desserts. I do my main business at either of the other two towns."

She was a little disappointed that there wasn't more here but she knew both Fredericksburg and Johnson City were really busy places and she could get anything she might need there. Not that she needed anything.

As he parked the truck in front of Dixie's Diner, she spotted a flash of color down the road. "What's that?"

"That is a new place just started last year. You know, the Wildflower Farms on the edge of Fredericksburg draws a ton of people to come look at all their wildflowers and to buy the seeds and take them home with them. Well, Martha and Amos got the idea that there was room for more than the one wildflower business and so they started up. It's a lot smaller but they do grow some beautiful flowers and their business is growing since they're right here on the main road. They're going to expand since they happened to own the land for generations and just wanted to see if they could compete. So far so good."

"That's really wonderful. I'm going to want to see it. And it's been a long time since I went to Wildflower Farms."

"Then I'll take you. This time of year, they have a lot blooming. And I have to run to Fredericksburg to see my lawyer, so that will be a good time to go."

"Perfect. You just tell me when and I'll clear my calendar."

They both laughed and didn't get out of the truck.

"You know, you live in a pretty neat area."

"It is. Most of the ranches have been here a lot of years. Some are selling out as the kids grow up and don't want to take over, so hands are changing."

"Gladly not yours, though."

"Thanks to you."

They stared at each other and a feeling of companionship filled the truck. She liked it. She realized she'd not actually felt this close to a man, ever.

He pulled his gaze from her and looked down the street before returning his gaze to her. "It's a good place. Although, I have to tell you it's not the greatest place if you're a guy looking to marry. There are fewer women in this place than men, being that it's a ranching community. You can imagine there's a lot more cowboys than women."

"Really? Is that why you're not married? Well, I mean weren't married." She smiled at him and the sun-bronzed skin around his eyes crinkled.

"Yeah, don't forget you married me. But no, that wasn't the reason. Okay, here it is. I've been burned by women more times than I care to look back on. They all seemed more interested in what I had to bring to the table—the money, not me as a person. I got tired of it. And then I met Delta. She conned me so bad, twisted me around her finger and had me thinking marriage. Then I found out she had another fella on the side and I was just the bank account. I've been sour ever since. And I don't talk about her, ever. So, now you know."

He'd been hurt. Really hurt. "You cared for her." It wasn't a question. She could tell he had. She wouldn't have had the power to hurt him like this if he hadn't.

"Yes, and I was a fool. I'm not keen on being a fool."

No, he wouldn't be. "I've been a fool, too, so don't feel like you're alone. Thankfully, Ginny has kept me from being a fool in trouble."

"I really like your friend Ginny and am glad you've had her helping you out."

She smiled. "Her and Loretta."

"That's really a scary thought." He shook his head. "Are you ready to eat? I have to go down to the feed store and pick up a few things but we never ate lunch and wrestling with calves makes a man hungry."

"Food sounds good."

They climbed from the truck just as a woman strode out of the antique store down the sidewalk. She was headed to the diner, too, it appeared.

An older woman, she wore jeans, boots, and a Western shirt. Her gray hair was pulled back in a long ponytail that hung down her back. She wasn't a big woman but had the leathered skin of a woman who'd spent time outside working. Allie knew a person could get that leathered look by sitting too long by a pool, too, but this woman did not look as though she spent time relaxing by a pool. She hustled down the street with movements of a much younger woman. And the moment she spotted them, her face broke into a grin. It was hard to tell her age but Allie had a feeling she was younger than her leathered skin let on. Maybe seventy-five when her skin said eighty. Her sage-green eyes danced with merriment as she stopped on the sidewalk to look at Allie and Wade.

"Well, look here. I heard you brought a bride home. At long last. Wade, son, your granddaddy would be so happy."

Allie didn't say anything, just gave the woman a smile and looked at Wade for direction.

Wade was smiling and he reached out and gave the woman a hug. "Hey, Penny, good to see you. And yes, this is Allie. We got married just the other day. And what's this you mean, my granddaddy would be happy?"

Allie heard the wariness in his words and curiosity got to her. "Hi, Penny. It's nice to meet you."

"Likewise, young lady. You look like you can keep this young man in line. And Wade, as for your granddaddy being happy—well, I know everything about that will that you got three months ago. Your granddaddy discussed it with me. And just so you know, there are some things that you might have not known. We might need to talk."

Wade looked a little bit confused. "He discussed it with you? Penny, why didn't you tell me this? It's been three months. And what do you mean, you know some things about it that I don't know?"

Penny crossed her arms and gave him a grin. "He just discussed it with me. He thought that somebody close to the family needed to know all the particulars of it, aside from the lawyer. Even though him and Cal are—were great buddies. You know, son, there's some things you don't put on paper. And me being as good a friend to your granddaddy and grandma all these years, I'm the one he came to. Therefore, I know that this young lady is beautiful and nice and that she and you married for the benefit of inheriting your granddaddy's land. No negativity toward you, Allie. Actually, I'm excited about it. Son, you showed initiative, doing what your granddaddy asked you to do. Something I wasn't sure you would be able to make yourself do since you have such an aversion to wedding—just never showed much of an effort at getting there. He was worried about that."

"I know he was. Look, we're standing out here on the sidewalk discussing all this. We were about to have lunch. Want to join us?"

"Don't mind if I do. I was just heading there myself. Let's grab a booth at the back. I don't really reckon you want a lot of people overhearing this conversation. I don't think it would be right by Allie for a lot of people to know y'alls marriage particulars."

Wade nodded and stepped back to allow them both to move. "I agree wholeheartedly, Penny." He splayed his hand in a sweep to allow them to go forward. "After you, ladies."

Allie went along with the couple. Her curiosity was getting the better of her. It seemed that Wade's will from his granddaddy was getting a little more complicated than it already was. A man who left his grandson an ultimatum of three months to getting married or lose an entire, humongous, thousands of acres and millions or even more dollars' worth of land and property—in her mind, well, to her it sounded as if he had something missing up there. But from what everyone said, he did it out of concern. But whatever the reason, she was along for the ride and growing closer to Wade, and more and more curious about how this all played out for him. She wanted the best for him. And she hoped that Penny wasn't about to tell him something he didn't want to hear.

They entered the diner. It was not packed considering it was now almost two o'clock. They had planned on having a late lunch and it certainly was. The waitress smiled at Wade and said hello in a manner that made Allie think she had at one time—or still did—wished or wanted more from Wade than the smile he gave her. It struck Allie then that as handsome as Wade was and as well known, he probably got that look from a lot of women. And that was part of his problem. It reminded her that when he had entered the truck stop and had been sitting at that table alone and looking so dejected, she had done something for him that was probably refreshing: she had asked out of concern whether he was okay. Maybe he'd sensed she hadn't had an ulterior motive behind her sincere question. Or just been so desperate he would have told anyone his problem. She wanted to believe it was a reaction to her specifically. And that was a growing problem for her because three months would be the end of her relationship with him.

She was glad that she knew nothing about him. But she knew herself well enough to know that his money would not have made a difference about how she'd reacted to him.

Once they'd slid into the booth, Penny didn't waste any time. She looked up at the waitress. "Carla, I'll have my usual and today I'm going to splurge and have half a glass of sweet tea in my unsweet. I'm celebrating Wade and Allie gettin' married."

The waitress smiled but it looked as if she were in pain at the effort. "You got married?" She let out a breath and then forced her smile to widen. "That's real nice. I guess the good ones always do. Congratulations."

Allie actually felt sorry for the woman.

"Thank you," Wade said, giving his attention to Allie. "I think I did well. This is Allie."

Carla handled it well, though Allie saw the skin around her mouth stiffen as she forced her smile wider. "Nice to meet you. Can I take your order?"

And the uncomfortable situation was over. Wade ordered a chicken fried steak with mashed potatoes and black-eyed peas. "They have the best chicken fried steak in the state as far as I'm concerned."

She glanced at the menu and looked up at Carla. "I couldn't eat the chicken fried steak—it's a little bit heavy for me. But I'd like to try that club sandwich if at all possible."

Carla tapped her pen on the pad she was holding and then gave her a small smile that didn't quite reach her eyes. "I'll put that down and that would actually be my choice, too. They make a good club sandwich. The bacon's fresh and so is the tomato. It's from the garden."

With that said, she headed to the back and Penny started talking. She'd cupped her hands on the table. "Okay, you two, so here's the deal. Your granddaddy made those slightly odd stipulations about you getting married to inherit the ranch and as you know, it was for your own good. He just wanted great-grandkids on that property. And he knows good and well that you just could have married her for the three-month time frame and then you two could divorce and go on your merry ways, go on about your business, both of you having gotten what you wanted—Allie getting the paycheck she's going to get and you getting the property and the money. And to be honest, your granddaddy knows that you worked your butt off to help build this ranch. And he didn't want you not to get it. He also knew you well enough to figure you would find a way to marry somebody.

"But he knew you weren't just going to marry

somebody who didn't appeal to you in some way. And I suspect, from my own observations of watching you for the last three months and you hadn't married somebody until right up to the deadline, that you had many a chance to offer the deal to a young woman and had yet to do it. I was starting to get a little bit concerned myself. And I imagine your granddaddy up in heaven was worrying, too, but you came through. I suspect there was a reason why you asked Allie to marry you. Now, don't say anything. I see that speculation in your eyes and when you look at Allie, I see a little twinkle there. But I think that like your granddaddy suspected, I, too, hoped that there was a little something between you two that got you both to agree to this marriage and that it was not just the money factor.

"So here's the deal: you know that it had a three-month time period but his hope was that in three months you two might find something more between you. And the old charmer hoped you'd find love. He was always a romantic when you got past the rough edges of him. Your grandmother testified to that many times to me."

Allie looked at Wade. They were sitting with their shoulders touching and she'd felt him tense.

"I had figured it was something like that." He didn't look happy. "But whatever he was thinking, I still don't agree with what he's done. But it's his will and in the end, he's been quite clear showing me that it is his land to do with as he wants, no matter how hard I worked."

She hurt for him.

"That's your view. And I'm not saying I agreed with him, either. But what's done is done, and you two are now on a journey to make it right—however you decide it will end for the two of you as a couple."

Their food arrived and they waited as Carla set the plates in front of them.

When she'd gone, Penny picked up her sandwich. "It is my dearest hope that you wouldn't just look at this like a paycheck—that you would at least give it a chance, a real chance. Therefore, I hope that you two get close to each other and drop your defenses." She looked at Allie. "I have a feeling you have some. I know Wade does. That boy is so tight-lipped and he's got his heart so bolted up it can't see daylight. And I understand why. For instance, I see how Carla eyed him. I understand it happens a lot and he's not just known here in this area for who and what he has. I'm sure you've looked him up by now and seen his picture is splayed everywhere. All the McCoy boys are. But Wade dislikes it the most, I think. He's wary. And that means I hope you two will be vulnerable with each other and honest."

Wade had listened quietly. Now he took a deep breath. "Penny, here's the deal. Allie is a good person and I'm not going to do anything that's going to hurt her. And what you're asking of us to do has the potential of backlash and backlash does damage. This is a business transaction as it stands now. If we change that, then Allie could get hurt. I could, too, but it's not me I'm worried about anymore. She's done this for me—yes, for the paycheck that she needs—but mostly out of the kindness of her heart. I'm not planning on toying with it."

Allie bit the inside of her lip as she contemplated

what he was saying. There was that small hope inside her that was suddenly wishing that they could give this a chance. Even if he was poor as dirt she'd want to, because Wade was a good guy and it wasn't because of what he had. He was just a good guy and she was overwhelmingly attracted to him like no man she'd ever been attracted to. And maybe it was just because he was giving her a chance to find a sanctuary for a little while from all of the troubles she had before.

But he was right in many ways. She was more vulnerable than him and she could get really hurt if they allowed this attraction they were feeling to go any further. Because she had no doubt that Wade would walk away. Her deadline was three months and she was gone. And there was nothing in his attitude that led her to believe that anything she could do would change that…

Penny gave Wade a very pointed look. "I understand what you're saying, Wade. But that's what your granddaddy wanted. He wanted you to give this a chance. And so for that, I promised him I would do a few things that I would have done for you if this was a normal marriage. I'm throwing you two a wedding reception dance in two weeks. And I expect you to come and be on your best behavior as a married couple. All your neighbors have no idea about the will and will want to wish you well and meet your lovely bride. All you need to do is come with smiles on your faces and looking like a happily married couple cutting cake, and dancing the first dance, just like if this was the reception after your quickie marriage. What do you think about that?"

Allie was dumbfounded. Stunned. Sick to her stomach.

CHAPTER TEN

Wade stared at Penny, the woman who was like a grandmother to him. Had been there for his family always. He didn't like her idea at all. He was sitting beside Allie right now and she had accidently bumped his thigh with her thigh and heat had risen up through him instantly. He'd been fighting off his attraction to her harder than ever since the calf incident that morning.

Three days in and he was struggling. He was attracted to Allie but that didn't mean he was going to fall in love with Allie. He wasn't going to let that happen. He had his reasons and he tried to explain, but he did not want to hurt Allie and he had this big fear that he would. And now Penny was really messing with his plan. But there was no getting around it. Penny got what Penny wanted.

"Penny, you are driving me crazy but okay. We're going to come because I know you and Granddaddy had a plan and we're going to see this thing through. Is that fine with you, Allie?"

She was biting the inside of her lip, and her eyes were very serious. "I am, but I thought I was going to come here and learn a few things on the ranch, and you know, play married until we parted ways. I hadn't planned on having to truly lie to anybody. Until right now, it hadn't hit me that all your friends and neighbors will be wanting to congratulate you. That will be lying. Face-to-face lying. I'm assuming you'll invite all the important people in Wade's business and people in his granddaddy's life?" Penny nodded.

Allie took a deep breath and Wade could feel her turmoil. But he didn't know what to do for her.

"Then that means we're really going to be lying to them. And that makes me uncomfortable. I'm not good at lying. Never have been and I don't like it. That's probably why I'm so terrible at it and always fell for whatever lies a fella felt like telling me."

Wade lost his appetite. She looked really panicked. She was so panicked she had clasped her hands together on the table around the front of her plate and her knuckles were white.

He placed a hand on top of hers. "Relax, Allie. Come on, breathe. Don't get all uptight and nervous. We're not going to be lying to them. Let's just say that for the night of the wedding reception, we give it our all just like Granddaddy wanted. It won't be like we're flat out lying that way—we're at least giving it a shot. What do you think about that? Will that help you?" *What was he committing to?*

"I know you don't want to and I understand. I respect that you don't want to lie to me either or lead me on. It's just so much more complicated than I thought when I married you. I thought it was cut-and-dried. I had no idea."

"Sugar," Penny smiled sympathetically at her, "I like you. I can tell you right now Wade's granddaddy would've liked you and his grandmother, too. You are very honest and wear your heart on your sleeve. That's a little bit dangerous but it means you are hoping for goodness. I'm going to come out and tell you, one woman to another, in this situation you might need to cover your heart up just a little bit. If at all possible. I can understand if you can't and I can understand where Wade's coming from too. He doesn't want to hurt you, and I can see what he's talking about now. But I don't see what it's going to hurt to truly give it a shot, like Wade's suggesting, for that night. And that won't be lying; it would just be between all of us. What do you say?"

Their gazes locked.

"Okay. I'm in. Let's do this," Allie said.

Her hands beneath his trembled just a little bit and only then did Wade realize he was still holding her hands. He could dive into those pools of blue. Because he knew Penny was seeing it all and Allie had no clue that she was already in trouble. Wade groaned inwardly and pulled his hand away from hers. He sounded conceited by knowing she was falling for him but it was right there on her face. It didn't take a genius to figure it out. Now he was in trouble because the thought of holding her in his arms while dancing appealed to him too much.

Allie stared out across the pasture at the horses running and frolicking with the colts. It was beautiful. The grass was so green and rich and the horses were amazing. There were eight horses and six babies. The prettiest one was a golden color with a cream mane that ruffled in the wind as it galloped across the pasture.

She made the call while she was standing there and checked on her mother. She was still the same. Allie planned to go see her the next week just to satisfy herself that all was well. She needed to ask Wade about either driving or taking the plane he had insisted she think of as hers while she was here. She hadn't missed the *while she was here* statement.

Since their lunch with Penny, Wade had shown her again how to feed the calves, and had approved that she could do it. She'd been so proud of that and had to fight down the want to hug him. But he'd been more reserved this time than the first, as if he were trying to keep her at arm's length, so she had made her excitement more reserved. He'd been working long hours and hadn't come to sit with her on the swing at night. Though they did eat together. He had also given her the keys to his truck so that she could go exploring if she wanted. She had gone to Fredericksburg one day and walked the long, long main street area where there was shop after shop of things to buy. She'd eaten lunch alone at an outside table of a restaurant that had live music and she'd people watched. She'd given in to temptation and gone in one of the many ice cream shops and bought a scoop and a piece of fudge. She'd come home empty-handed.

"How did your day go?" Wade had asked that evening on his way to his office.

"It was nice. I enjoyed it. And your day, how was it?"

His gaze had been guarded. "We're moving cattle from a ravine and into a flatter pasture in case of flash floods. It was hot. I'm sorry, I need to finish up some paperwork for a group of cattle buyers."

"Sure. I'm going to swing then head to bed."

And then she'd taken her pad and pen out to the swing and he'd gone to his office.

Standing there watching the horses, she replayed every moment they'd spent together before he had closed himself off. What had gone wrong?

Four days had passed and she was going stir-crazy. And she missed seeing Wade. She'd been feeding the calves, after assuring him she could manage, and she had done okay.

As she stood there, a truck startled her as it barreled down the lane from the entrance gate. She was in a pasture to the back of the stables, so she wasn't sure whether the truck would see her but as she stood there, it angled onto the road that led straight to where she was, as if whoever was driving had spotted her standing there beside the horse pen.

The truck pulled to a stop and a woman a little older than her hopped out and strode toward her. "Hey there. Are you Allie?"

Allie walked toward the brunette curiosity driving her forward. She smiled. "I am. I'm married to Wade." She didn't know what else to say, but still not comfortable saying she was married to Wade.

"Great." A wide smile erupted over the woman's face. "I'm *really* glad to meet you. I'm Caroline McCoy. Wade's girl cousin-well second cousin to be accurate. Our granddaddies are brothers. Not that you'd confuse me with his boy cousins—my brothers—but I'm the only girl in the bunch. And I am so thrilled to see one of the boys tossing in the towel and settling down."

"Oh, that's nice." What else could she say? She didn't know why he and Allie had married. Allie realized Wade and his brothers hadn't told anyone about the will. Not even his cousins. It hit her then who Caroline was. "Oh, your parents died in the plane crash with Wade's parents?"

Caroline nodded. "Yes, Sadly, we lost them all far too early. So, we McCoy cousins have a bond we wish desperately we didn't have but we do and we're stronger because of it. I adore Wade, Todd and Morgan as if they were my brothers."

"I am so sorry for your loss. I lost my dad not too long ago and it's just hard." She couldn't bring herself to go deeper into her situation and her mother's struggles right now. It was too close to her heart.

"Thank you, and I'm so sorry about your dad. It's not easy, but now you have Wade to help you through this tough time."

"Yes," she said, knowing it was so true in so many ways.

Caroline smiled. "I came over to welcome you. I hope that Wade is treating you right."

There was teasing in her words and it made Allie laugh. "He is."

"I figured so, since he married you. That is a feat! I'm going to want to hear the specifics on that at some point. I mean, he hardly dates and then he goes on a cattle-buying road trip and brings home a wife too.

Were you dating and we didn't know?"

"Um, no. We met when he stopped at the truck stop I worked at."

To Caroline's credit, she just smiled. "Love at first sight. I love it. Well, I have been meaning to come over here and welcome you ever since I heard the news. You two must have had a whirlwind of a relationship."

"You could say that." Allie said as little as possible. From Caroline's comments, she wondered whether she thought they'd met at the truck stop on a different road trip and had dated at least a little while. If so, she wasn't going to deny or expand on what really happened.

"We need to hang out. Bond. I can help you acclimate to the area. And Penny called and told me she's throwing y'all a wedding bash. I think it's a fantastic idea. A reception with dancing and live music and cake, lots of rich and creamy cake. Anyway, she suggested you might need a girlfriend to help you navigate this shindig and I am always up for a party. And I wanted to meet you anyway, so our stars have collided. I'd have come over sooner but I was out of town. But never fear, I am here."

Allie liked her and she reminded her in many ways of Ginny, and she missed Ginny so very much. Their very short phone conversations hadn't been enough but they'd seemed to be playing phone tag. Caroline had that boldness that her friend had and Allie was drawn to that.

She really needed to go back to Tyler and see her mother and Ginny. She was going to talk to Wade tomorrow.

She relaxed. "I've actually been thinking I needed to figure out what to wear to the reception/dance. What am I supposed to wear to this shindig?" she asked, using Caroline's description. "Would you want to go shopping?" Allie didn't normally go shopping with someone she barely knew but she was actually a little bit desperate.

"The magic words. What are you doing this afternoon?"

"Um, well, nothing. Wade's working cows and Nelda's got the house sparkling and dinner already in the refrigerator and it's barely past lunch. And I've already fed the calves. To tell you the truth, I'm bored out of my mind."

A grin spread across Caroline's face. "Get your things and load up. We're going shopping for a fabulous dress and some girl time. There are some great specialty shops in Fredericksburg. Or we could go to San Antonio. That's the closest place you'll find a decent dress. So, we'll just have to leave your sweetheart a little note and tell him that I kidnapped you and are headed to Fredericksburg. If we can't find a perfect dress there, we'll just be forced to go shopping again." She laughed. "Tell him I said we would be back when we get back."

Allie chuckled, not exactly sure what to make of Caroline but she most assuredly reminded her of Ginny. Yes, it was time to go home and see her. She could invite Ginny to drive out here for the dance if she had time. Or maybe they could send that plane they owned for her because she probably wouldn't have the time to get away from her vineyard. Her work was everything to her. She decided tomorrow she would give Ginny a call.

"Then let's do it. I guess I need to change?"

"You're just fine. I don't know if you noticed, but I'm a jeans and T-shirt kind of gal. At least you have sandals on—I have my boots on. When we whip out the payment, they will take us however they can get us."

Yes, Ginny for certain. "Sounds good."

"I promise you, though, that I'll clean up for the dance. I do like frilly things too, just in their time. I just got off of riding my horses for the morning, so I might even stink a little bit. Hope you can take it." She laughed. "Just teasing. I took a shower before I came over here—I couldn't meet you for the first time smelling like my horses."

Allie laughed and knew she was going to get along with Caroline just fine.

They walked toward her truck. "I'll ride with you to the house and leave him that note."

"Hop in. Sounds like a plan to me."

A few minutes later, they were chatting like old friends as Caroline drove down the winding roads toward Fredericksburg.

"You really ran from the cops in a high-speed chase?" Allie asked after her question about cops patrolling the area, because Caroline was going a bit over the limit and at times caused Allie to hold tight to the edge of her seat. The woman drove as if there were a fire somewhere and they were the firetruck.

Caroline winked at her. "You are so easy for me to tease. No, I did not run from the cops but I thought about it. Jesse James Johnson—that's the deputy out of Stonewall—he and I don't get along too well. And when I see him, sometimes I tease him and that's what I was talking about. I speed a little to aggravate him. He doesn't always make it easy on me, though. He's threatened a time or two just to haul me in and have the book thrown at me."

"Why would he do that?" Allie didn't know whether she needed to ask for more explanation or whether she needed to decide right then and there that Caroline liked to pull her leg a lot. She would ask Wade about her when she saw him later that evening.

"Because I frustrate him. He thinks I'm a spoiled

brat and I think he's a good-looking hunk of a man who thinks just because he wears a uniform he can call all the shots. I told him to throw the book at me and I'd have his job."

"You told him that?" Allie was really confused and watching the road closely for any signs of a patrol SUV.

"I told him that just to rile him up." Caroline laughed. "He's kind of fun to rile up."

Allie was relieved when town came into view and traffic was ahead and Caroline eased her boot off the gas. "You really remind me of my friend Ginny. I think you and her would get along really well. Both of you kind of terrify me."

Caroline threw her head back and hooted. "Well, I might have to meet this Ginny because I don't think I've ever terrified anybody. Maybe I need to meet your friend so I can see what she does that reminds you of me. Maybe I'll need to calm myself down."

"Something tells me that that's probably not possible because I know it's not possible for Ginny."

"I was just teasing you, you know. My

granddaddy agrees with Jesse James—always tells me I'm a spoiled brat and one day somebody is going to take me serious and I'm going to be in a whole heap of trouble."

"Well, I hope it's not that deputy and you don't end up getting thrown into jail."

"Again, he wouldn't do that. Besides, he actually likes me and I don't know, but I think I like him too. But I'm not going to tell him—I'm just going to keep giving him a hard time."

Allie was thinking about the deputy with lights blazing in a high-speed car chase, chasing after Caroline. She got a picture of the way she teased Wade about chasing her across the pasture on his horse while she was on a runaway horse. The thought made her smile. She actually thought it would be quite exciting to be rescued like that by Wade. Maybe Caroline had a similar fantasy about this deputy with the name of an outlaw.

They made it to the main shopping area of town without having to be chased down or ending up in jail, and Allie was quite relieved. She followed Caroline into a store with very expensive-looking clothes. She paused in the doorway. She didn't have the money for this. Then reality hit her and she reminded herself she did have access to whatever she needed. It was a very odd feeling for her. Ever since her dad and mom's wreck, she had been so behind on everything. Her money troubles had been just so overwhelming and now to know that she could probably buy anything she wanted was a bit overwhelming too. But even knowing that she could didn't mean she would. She had a frugal heart and she was determined to only spend what she needed. But she also needed to make sure that she was dressed appropriately.

"Are you ready to shop till we drop?" Caroline turned and motioned for Allie to follow her.

"At least until we find the right dress. I hope we're able to find it quickly."

Caroline looked at her as though she had just said something horrible. "Quickly? Are you kidding me? We are going to try on every dress in this store and then we are going to move on to another one if you don't find anything. This is your wedding reception.

You need to look like a million bucks. You need to make my cousin Wade fall in love with you all over again."

She felt very deceptive suddenly because it was very obvious that Caroline did not realize that this was a fake marriage in every sense of the word. But the idea of making Wade fall in love with her was just wishful thinking. That would not happen. Still, she wouldn't mind seeing whether she could make him think about it at least.

"You are absolutely right," she said. "Let's do this."

CHAPTER ELEVEN

Wade came in that evening, hot and tired and a bit worried when he didn't find Allie anywhere. He looked through the house and then was headed back outside to look for her when he noticed a note on the counter. She'd gone shopping with Caroline. He rubbed his temple. His cousin was back in town. And taken Allie shopping for a dress for the reception. That should be fun for her, he hoped, as he headed to his office and the conference call with his brothers. He'd told them after he'd married Allie that he was married and they had still been mad that he'd had to get married to save the ranch.

He'd been too busy to worry about how they felt. He hoped tonight's call, a regular call to discuss any business, went better than that call to Morgan and visit to Todd had gone. He also planned to tell them about Penny and that she was throwing them the reception and that they'd need to be there. He didn't expect that to go over real well with Morgan. He'd think his chain was being yanked once again and he obviously had a real hang-up about that. Wade wasn't going to worry about it too much, though. His main concern right now, he realized with a grin, was wondering what Allie was going to look like in the dress she brought home for the party.

Allie had bought the most beautiful dress in the world. At the very least, the most beautiful dress she had ever owned. Wade had been in his office when she'd arrived back at the house and she stuck her head through the open doorway. He looked weary as he sat studying his computer.

"Honey, I'm home," she said, teasing him, feeling lighthearted and happy. *Happy*. The thought felt light on her heart and she took it while she could get it. Being with Caroline had made her a little bolder than she normally was, much like being with Ginny always had.

His eyes lit up at her voice and he instantly rose from the chair and moved around the desk toward her.

Butterflies lifted through her.

"Great. Did you have fun? I'm afraid to ask what Caroline might have gotten you mixed up in. I was just glad I didn't have to come bail you two out of Jesse James's jail cell."

She laughed. "She told me about that. I'm really glad you didn't have to do that either. She drives like a race car driver."

"Like a moonshiner, you mean?"

"Exactly. Thankfully, we did not see this Jesse James, although I was curious about him."

Wade stood in front of her, grinning down at her, and she tingled all over just being near him. *Gee whizz, she was in a bad way.*

"You'll meet him at the party next week, I'm sure. Him and a horde of other friends. I'm really sorry you have to go through that."

She refused to get down about the party and that it didn't matter whether she met his friends and family considering she wasn't going to be here long enough to get their names straight. "It'll be fun. And I got the most wonderful dress. I'm going to feel like a princess. Caroline made me get it when I thought it was too much."

"Good for her. You had the money—you used the card I gave you, right?"

"Yes, I remembered it and since this was for our party, I used it. But I still felt weird. But that's not what I meant about the dress being too much. I meant too much, too over the top—you know…too fancy for me."

His brows crinkled like they often did over his serious eyes. "Nothing is too fancy for you. I don't like it when you think less of yourself. You are as good as anyone and gorgeous without the dress."

She swallowed the lump in her throat. She hadn't

meant to draw sympathy or compliments with her comment. It had just been a comment, a normal thought, and she hadn't meant anything by it. But he had jumped in there defensively for her. The idea touched her deeply and she was speechless.

He touched her chin. "I have known you for just a short while but I have a feeling you talk negatively about yourself all the time. You need to stop that. I saw a poster somewhere that said be kind to yourself first and it rubs off on everyone around you. You're already kind to others—think how much more amazing you'll be when you're kinder to yourself first."

Her mouth dropped open. She let out a small laugh of wonder. "If you are trying to build up my ego and self-esteem, you are doing a great job. You should go into business."

His eyes danced with merriment. "You've turned up in my life and are a full-time job. If you ease up on yourself and I see progress, then maybe I'll think about it later." He chuckled.

She did too and they ended up standing there, grinning at each other.

"You going to show me that dress?" he drawled after a long, dangerous moment.

A moment in which Allie had to fight the want to throw her arms around him and feel the security and wonderful feel of his body against hers. Then kiss those smiling, tempting lips of his.

Goodness, maybe she might not need to hang out with Caroline anymore; she was feeling way too bold at the moment. Of course, she didn't—wouldn't—do such a thing...but she sure had been thinking about it.

"Not until the party. Sorry." She loved the way his eyes danced at her words.

"I guess you're going to make me suffer?"

Since they were teasing, she went along with it. She placed a finger on his chest and tapped lightly. "Sure thing, cowboy." And then, unable to keep up the ruse, she laughed and spun away and headed down the hall. "I'm thinking I might not need to hang out with your cousin. She's rubbing off on me."

"I like it, so don't stop on my account," he called then chuckled. "You going to bed?"

She turned at the end of the hall. "Yes, and I need

to put my things away. Shopping till you drop is not just a saying, you know. It's the truth. I'm about ready to pass out. Goodnight."

"Goodnight. Sweet dreams."

His words followed her and sure enough, her dreams were sweet. She dreamed that she had met Wade at a picnic and fallen in love. And that this was real and not a business deal.

Nelda was just getting off her cell phone when Wade came in from the barn. She looked worried.

"Nelda, what's wrong?"

Allie came in from the living room. "Nelda, are you okay?"

"My mother had a fall. She's okay. But it scared me. She didn't break her hip but I'm always scared she might. She's ninety years old and still working in her garden. Anyway, I'm a bit frazzled. I hate to ask but I'm going to need to go down there for a few days. Help out at the hospital and get her home. She's bruised her hip, so I'm not sure how bad. Or what she'll need until I get there."

"You go. Take all the time you need. Can we take you in the plane?"

"No, but thank you. I'll need my car and it's just a few hours to Waco."

"Okay then, but anything you need, let me know. We'll call this paid leave. Take—"

"No, I can't ask that."

"You aren't asking. You and Roland help keep this place—me—running. I'm grateful for you. Go, spend time with your mother. Don't worry about us. We can make it on our own for a while. But don't go thinking we don't need you. Right, Allie?"

Allie nodded. "He's right. Give your mother our well wishes and don't worry about us. I will cook for this man and he will smile, eating whatever I put in front of him."

Nelda laughed. "That sounds interesting." She winked. "You two enjoy some alone time. Newlyweds need that. Okay, I better go call Roland and then head out."

"If he needs to go with you, he can."

"No, he will drive me batty wandering around a hospital with nothing to do. You keep him, please."

Wade grinned. "I see your point. I'll do that."

Allie hugged the older woman and he did, too, and then they walked out to her car with her and watched as she drove away. When he looked down at Allie, he saw worry on her mind.

"What's wrong?" He dipped his head to meet her gaze.

"I am so sorry for her mother. But it made me think and I was going to mention it, I need to go home to check on Mama too."

"Yes, you do. I'll tell you what, how about I call and have the pilot get the plane ready and we go down there for the day. Or two. Clay and Roland can handle things here for me."

"You want to come with me? Won't you be restless at the rehab?"

"I want to come with you. And I'd like to check everything out too. Make sure there isn't something more we can do."

Tears filled her eyes and she threw her arms

around him. "Thank you. You are such a kind man."

He caught her to him, feeling grateful that he could help her and be there for her.

Allie stared out the window of the small jet. She couldn't believe this was her life. "Do you own this?" She couldn't help asking the question. It was just so out of her realm to be sitting here, flying toward home.

"No, not completely. Granddaddy figured out early on that he preferred being able to pick up a phone and have a plane here in less than an hour. It worked better for our needs, so he invested in the company my cousin owns and we have access when we need it. I don't fly as much as Todd or anywhere near as much as Morgan but if we need to head different directions on the same day we can arrange it."

"Oh." The lifestyle was so beyond her. He was sitting beside her and leaned close to look over her shoulder. He smelled so very wonderful. "Thank you again for going with me. It means a lot." She meant it.

Wade's gray-blue gaze held steady. "I'm glad you let me tag along." His hand lifted and cupped her jaw, so very tenderly. "You doing okay with missing your dad?"

She swallowed hard. That he would think to ask about her grief touched her deeply, something he was beginning to do on a regular basis. He was asking about hers and she hadn't asked about how he was doing.

"I am. I miss him so. It hits me out of nowhere sometimes and then other times I'll have a really good day, like yesterday and today, and I won't even think about him and then I feel guilty. How about you? I'm so sorry I haven't asked."

"I'm doing fine. I miss Granddaddy but I guess we can't stop time from marching on. Besides, he's still here in a way, giving orders and making himself known." He grinned and then it wavered. "I'm glad I met you, Allie. This isn't exactly what he had in mind, I don't think, but this little scheme he concocted has enabled me to meet you and I hope to help you.

Because you've helped me immensely."

"I'm glad. I wish I had met him. He seemed like a very good grandfather. He loved his boys a lot because he wanted something more for y'all."

He looked thoughtful. "Something more. Yes, that's exactly what he wanted. Money isn't everything. He knew that. Now, enough about me—I asked you first. How are you doing?"

His thumb gently caressed her cheek and she wished his hand would remain right there always. She was surprised he hadn't let it drop away already. They were flying high above the Earth at hundreds of miles an hour and her heart was racing by at the speed of light.

"I'm doing good. I'm excited to see my mom, even though she won't know me, won't even know I'm there. But still, I'll get to hold her hand and feel her soft skin and talk to her like I did every day before…I moved to the ranch with you." She sniffed. "Sorry, didn't mean to get emotional. I thought I had a handle on it. I'm just so glad to get to see her."

He looked troubled and dropped his hand. Then he reached for her hand. "Allie, I am so sorry. What a jerk I've been. I've moved you across Texas and you need to be near your mother. She needs you."

"The doctors said I didn't need to be there every day."

"I don't care what they said; you want to be there every day. What if we get her moved closer to us?"

She was speechless. "But it's only for three months."

"Less than that now. But what if she wakes up and you can't get there fast enough? Because you're going to want to be there in five minutes. I know I would want to. No, I've gone about this all wrong."

"But, it might not be good to move her."

"You leave that to me. I'll check everything out while you're in there spending time with her. And then you and the doctors can make the decision. But at least you'll have all the options."

"I-I don't know what to say. This is more than I could ask for. Thank you."

"You don't have to thank me. Allie, I should have thought about this already."

"Maybe so, if you say so, but I never imagined it a possibility until now. We just live in such different stratospheres." And although very grateful for what he was attempting to do, it was never more apparent that they did live in different worlds.

CHAPTER TWELVE

Wade was an idiot. How had he taken Allie away from her mother as ill as she was and not even thought about having her transferred to a top-ranked facility in San Antonio or Austin area? *How had he asked that of her? He had taken care of all her expenses, rent, car payments, everything but he'd not thought about transferring her closer to Allie.*

When they reached the rehab center in Tyler, he went in with Allie to check on her mother. His heart clenched looking at the small woman lying in the bed. She was small like Allie and the resemblance was striking. But where Allie was vibrant and alive-looking, her mother was deathly pale and immobile.

"Hello, Mama," Allie said, softly, taking her hand ever so carefully in hers. "I'm sorry I've been gone all week. You look good, though. And I brought my husband, Wade, to see you. We're going to try to move you closer to us so I can come see you more. Isn't that great?"

Her voice trembled and he slipped his hand onto Allie's shoulder and squeezed gently. Leaning forward, he spoke softly. "If you're okay, then I'm going to let you sit here and just visit and I'll go get started on seeing what we can do."

She nodded. "Thanks."

He passed Ginny in the hallway.

She paused to look at him. "I have to give you credit. You're not as dumb as I took you for. This is a good thing. They don't know if Mrs. Jordan is going to pull out of this. If something happens to her while Allie is at your place, it will kill Allie that she's not here close and hadn't seen her mother. I mean, you might be distracting her with your ranch and all that, but there is a part of her that needs to be there for her mother. I applaud you that you've realized that." She tipped her lime-green hat at him and then strode down the hall and into the room with Allie.

Wade hadn't even had time to say anything. He was just thankful that he had overcome his dumbness and hopefully got this fixed because everything Ginny said was true.

By the time they arrived home that night, it was late. Allie was exhausted, amazed, and thankful. Her mother was still holding her own, with no changes though. However, the doctors had given the okay for her to be moved to a rehab facility that was little over an hour away from her. It came highly recommended and she would get excellent care there and Allie could go every day to see her if she wanted. Wade had made it all possible and she was being transported the following week when the room would be ready for her. He had assured her if her mother hadn't come out of her coma by the end of their three-month contract, he would have her transported back to Tyler or wherever Allie wanted to take her.

She was still confused by that but the main thing was she would have her mother close again. Ginny, to Allie's shock, had said Wade had done good. And that was high praise coming from a sharp-tongued Texas gal.

When they finally walked inside the house and walked down the hall to their rooms, Wade paused at her doorway. "You look weary. I hope you get some sleep and that this helps ease more stress off your shoulders."

She looked at him. "Thank you. It does. But, Wade, you know you won't always be able to keep the stress off my shoulders. Besides, I'm tougher than I look and tougher than I get credit for."

He smiled. "I know that. I happen to think you're one of the strongest people I know. You're quiet about it but you've got grit, and that was evident from the first moment I met you."

"Really?"

He cupped her chin. "Really." And then he kissed

the tip of her nose. "Now go get your sleep."

Allie slipped into her room but didn't go directly to sleep. Instead, after showering and slipping on a pair of sleeping shorts with matching shirt, she curled into the thick plush chair near the large window of her room and stared up at the huge moon and let the emotions she'd been struggling to control release. She had known Wade McCoy for such a short time, and yet, her heart was already in danger.

She would never be able to repay him for what he'd done for her. And it felt odd being in a relationship so lopsided. But, she reminded herself, she wasn't really in a relationship. She was in a business transaction and he had told her he would do whatever was needed for her mother because she'd married him. And he'd done that.

It might not have been personal. But it had felt personal.

So what was she supposed to do?

Wade hadn't slept well. He'd had his wife on his mind.

His wife who was sleeping in the room across the hallway. He told himself thinking of her as his wife was walking in dangerous territory. But yesterday she had felt like his wife. It had felt good to do something for her that was meaningful. He hadn't really ever felt that before. Not like that.

He walked into the kitchen earlier than usual because he couldn't take lying there any longer. He stopped short when he found Allie at the stove with her back to him as she fried bacon in a skillet and hummed softly as she worked. The table was set and there was even a small vase holding a couple of roses from the bushes outside by the patio. His heart stumbled and a feeling of contentment stole over him. It was so strong that he had to force himself to swallow the lump in his throat. He had the almost overwhelming need to walk up behind her, press a kiss to her neck and put his arms around her and whisper good morning in her ear. In his vision, she spun in his arms, and planted a kiss on his lips then murmured good morning to him.

He must have made some kind of noise or she just sensed him because she turned and smiled. "Good morning. I thought I'd show you my skills while I could and try to show my gratitude for yesterday."

Move. He stepped into the room and walked toward the coffeepot. "It smells amazing. I didn't even think anything about it until I walked in and spotted you. Nelda is always here frying bacon, so my brain...anyway, you look good—I mean, at home in the kitchen." *Did women take it as an insult if you told them they looked good in the kitchen?* He didn't want to insult her but she did. And she looked as if she liked being there. He filled the mug of coffee to give his hands something to do because they were itching to wrap themselves around her waist or to take her hand and tug her close. He took a sip of coffee and studied her over the brim. "You don't owe me anything. Like I said, it was part of the deal. And, I should have done it sooner."

She breathed deeply then smiled. "I won't keep harping on it then." She turned back to the stove and began moving the bacon to a plate covered with napkins. Then she stepped over to the oven and pulled the door open. After grabbing a mitten from the counter, she pulled a tray of biscuits from the oven and something else…cinnamon rolls. He'd smelled cinnamon lightly but once she'd opened the oven door, the scent filled the room and his stomach growled.

"I wasn't sure if you like cinnamon rolls, so I made biscuits too."

"You are showing off. I love both."

She smiled. "Wonderful. Ginny's grandmother taught both of us how to make these and I can't take credit for what you are about to experience. They are amazing."

He grinned. "You baked them."

"Yes, I did. But it's the technique and the ingredients that make them. Both I got from Mimi—that's Ginny's grandmother's name—and if the way to a man's heart is through his stomach, you are about to fall in love with her."

He wasn't sure about her logic but a few moments later, when he bit into that cinnamon roll, he knew it was true: if the stomach was the way to his heart, he could definitely fall in love. But it wouldn't be with Mimi. It would be with the one who'd taken the time to bake them just for him.

"What'd I tell you?" She beamed at him from her chair then took a bite of one herself. "Mmm, that is so good."

He took another bite and felt as though his mouth had gone to heaven. "You should open a bakery."

She laughed. "Not with the hours they keep. No, thank you. I just plan to amaze my kids and husband one day...I mean, my real husband. The one I'm going to have kids with one day."

He stopped eating. "Right." He lost his appetite. "They'll be lucky to have you. Doing that," he managed.

She smiled. "Thanks." She set the last of her cinnamon roll down and looked down, as if thinking.

"Allie, do you mind if I ask why you were working at the truck stop? I mean, nothing wrong with it but I'm just wondering." She could have been baking, if nothing else. Even though she didn't act as though that was something she'd wanted to do.

She looked hesitant. "Well, it was a job that worked for me while I was spending so much time at the hospital with Mama. And I'd waitressed there part-time when I was in college. After my florist shop I owned burned down."

"You owned a florist shop and it burned down?"

"Yes, not too long before my parents' wreck."

"It all hit about the same time." He looked at her curiously. "Why didn't you build your business back?"

"Because I didn't have the money to build back. Anyway, that was the past. I guess I better go feed my babies. Are you going out in the field today?"

"I am. Do you want to come?" She had avoided answering all of his questions. *What had happened?* Because something told him there was more to the story.

Her head came up. "Yes. That would be great. I promise not to get in the way."

He liked seeing her excitement. "You won't be. We'll go on the four-wheeler, if you don't mind riding with me."

"No, I don't. But why not the horse?"

"Because they're moving the horses out of a ravine and it just works better for me for this job. Plus,

I don't want you on a horse by yourself in that area. I'd rather have you with me." He held her gaze. He didn't want her on a horse because he wanted her on the four-wheeler holding on to him. He had a problem and it was that he wanted to feel her arms around him. And if this was the only way, then so be it.

CHAPTER THIRTEEN

The night of the party, Allie stood in front of the mirror and studied herself. It was a little more daring than what she normally would have bought but Caroline had really urged her to buy it. And in reality, she really loved the dress. The neck dipped down just a little bit farther than what she would normally wear but it wasn't indecent. It just had the most beautiful skirt that swirled around her ankles, and they had bought a beautiful pair of shoes to go with it, the heels a little bit higher than she normally wore. And Caroline was going to come over and help her do her hair.

She had been shocked to know that Caroline, as much of a cowgirl as she was, said she was really good with hair. Allie was so nervous that she would take any help she could get and it was nice knowing that Caroline was in her corner. She stared at the dress that she was holding on its hanger in front of her and wondered what Wade would think of the dress. She'd been thinking about that a lot. She'd been thinking about him all the time. They'd had a wonderful week, but it had been filled with tension. She thought he was feeling emotions toward her and she knew she was feeling things for him that were going to make it so hard to leave when he let her go.

Would he let her go?

He'd said he would and nothing she'd said this week had had him saying otherwise. They had officially made it a month and still had two to go. She could only hope that during that time he might fall for her like she had fallen for him.

She heard the doorbell and she laid the dress on the bed and hurried downstairs to let Caroline in. She was in Wade's bedroom with the dress, having to go through the charade even with Caroline that they were actually married. She felt bad about the lie but it really wasn't anyone's business, so she didn't feel terrible.

She swung the door open and Caroline stood there with her hand on her hip, grinning at her. Caroline wore a beautiful silver dress that she had bought that had no swirling skirt; it was just straight and came right below her mid-calf. She wore a pair of glittery heels with it that made her look like a million bucks. Allie couldn't help but be a little bit startled; she had seen her in the dress when they were shopping but now Caroline had pulled her hair up in a very careless but cascading look and she had applied her makeup beautifully. She was stunning.

"Come in. You look gorgeous. I'm so nervous, I can't hardly stand it. Wade's not here yet. He's running late, but he said it wouldn't take him long to get dressed. They had some kind of emergency and needed him somewhere—in the south pasture or something like that. They've been moving a lot of cattle lately."

"There's always something. So just get used to it.

But if he says he'll be here, he'll be here. That's one thing about Wade—he usually always does what he said he was going to. I've never known him to really deviate from that. He's very reliable."

As they headed up the stairs, Allie's mind stuck on Wade. She was falling for him and tonight they were going to pretend they were really married for the benefit of all the people at the reception. She was the one who had wanted this and now she wasn't sure she could handle it. He was going to hold her in his arms and dance with her. She thought of the day that she'd ridden the four-wheeler with him to herd cattle. She'd had to hold on to him pretty much the entire time and by the end of the day she had barely been able to not throw herself at him and beg him to kiss her. Because she couldn't trust herself, she'd run to her room as quickly as possible, saying she was worn out. And she had been—worn out from wanting him to kiss her.

How was she going to hide her feelings tonight?

"Okay, girlie. Sit down here." Caroline patted the chair in front of the bathroom mirror.

Allie sat down and looked at Caroline in the

mirror. "What are you going to do to it? I've never actually worn my hair up before. I mean, I've pulled it up in a ponytail but like dressy—I've never done that. Yours is beautiful but I think that's a little too much for me, don't you think?"

Caroline gave her the *are-you-kidding-me* look in the mirror. She picked up the curling iron that Allie had heated up. "You just let me do this hair. Actually, I don't know what I'm going to do until I get started. But we're going to do some long curls and put a little bit of it up at least. That will make you look all sexy and everything. This is, after all, a wedding reception party—you want an updo, just like you would have done if you were getting married. I can tell you that if Wade's granddaddy was still alive, he would have thrown you a party. A huge party. Penny is trying her best to do it up like he would have. But it will be hard to do."

"Really?"

"Oh yeah. This ranch has seen some monstrous parties. Great Uncle J.D. loved a good party and through the years, they got bigger. But when we were younger and they were simpler, he would string lights across the decks and they'd clean out one of the stables and have huge dances when me and the boys were growing up. And I can tell you, Wade knows how to dance. So do his brothers. Morgan is a really good dancer but Wade and Todd can burn it up too. Wade, he's a good two-stepper. You'll have fun. And he can waltz, too. Have you already danced with him?"

Allie's stomach felt a little wobbly and the butterflies were nose-diving in her chest just thinking about dancing with him. She felt a little hot all over. "No, I haven't and I'm not a very good dancer."

Caroline smiled. "He'll teach you. You just let him do the leading and you'll be fine."

She watched Caroline as she finished curling the different strands of hair in big looping curls that, when she let them go, hung down Allie's back in soft, gentle waves. It made her eyes look even bigger but the end result she liked, even though she was a little bit uncomfortable.

"Ta-da," Caroline sang. "We're done. You look amazing. Wade is going to be one happy fella."

Allie stared at herself and her hand touched the exposed section of her neck. "I do look a little different, don't I?"

"You look beautiful. Like Cinderella looking for her fella." Caroline slapped a hand to her hip. "Something tells me you don't believe that."

"I never have had much confidence. But you—you made me beautiful."

"No, I enhanced what the good Lord gave you. Everyone can enhance."

Allie sighed. "I'm really nervous."

"Nothing wrong with nerves. Just don't give in to them. Now go put that dress on."

She went to the next room, slipped into the dress and then put the shoes on. Caroline had done such an amazing job with her hair so she put a layer of base on, not needing much because being in the sun had given her skin a golden glow. She put a little extra blush on, then mascara, and finished with a little lip gloss. And then she stared at herself. She felt a little bit like a fairy-tale princess. She told herself that was a silly way to feel. But she could not get rid of the feeling that

Wade was like a fairy-tale prince to her. She'd been in such a situation and he had waltzed into that truck stop and changed her life. At least for now.

Wade was running late. He had brought the truck to a screeching halt and practically dove out of the truck and hit the gravel jogging. His boots pounded on the gravel; then the grass and in seconds he was on the patio. He had the back door open within thirty seconds of pulling to a halt by the house. This was supposed to be their wedding reception dance party—or whatever the heck they called it—and he was running late. She hadn't said anything but he thought Allie was really looking forward to tonight. He was and he wasn't. He would get to hold her, using dancing as an excuse. He wasn't too late yet but if he didn't get changed and showered quick, he would be. He stripped off his shirt in the washroom, yanked his work boots off and left them in the hallway. As he practically jogged through the living area of the house in his socked feet, he wondered where Allie was. He knew Caroline was coming to do her hair, so he assumed she was probably already dressed as he jogged up the staircase.

He called out to her, "Allie, I'm home. Where are you?" He did a tap on the guest door and pushed it open. "Allie, are you in here?" No answer. *Maybe she was outside on the back porch or maybe she had gone with Caroline*. Surely not. *Maybe she was in his room*. He opened the door and stopped short. "Allie," he said, stunned.

Allie stood in the center of his room, looking like a vision straight out of one of those magazines. She had her back to him as he walked in and as she spun toward him, the skirt swirled about her legs, emphasizing her small waist and her gracefulness. Her big eyes met his and took his breath away. He had startled her and she'd gasped and her hand went to her heart. He smiled. His stomach felt as if he had a flock of birds going crazy in it. "You look beautiful." He pretty much gasped himself. He was not doing well when it came to words.

"You made it," she said, her voice breathless. "You startled me. And I don't know why. I should've been ready for you."

"Wow, you take my breath away." His muddled brain was spinning and his mouth had gone dry.

She smiled, almost shyly. "Thank you. I was hoping you would like it. I didn't want to go to this and embarrass you."

He crossed to her. He would've touched her but he had been working cows all day. "Darlin', you would never embarrass me. Distract me and tempt me to make us late by kissing you breathless, yes. I better quit gawking at you and get in there and get changed before Penny has my hide for getting you to the party late."

She laughed. "Okay. I'll go downstairs and wait for you. I probably don't need to be here when you come busting out of there without your clothes on." Her gaze dropped to his bare chest and everything in him seized up. She blushed and then spun and pretty much raced for the door.

He hurried and jumped in the shower. Within just a few minutes, he had showered, added cologne, shaved fast, combed his hair, and then went in the closet and figured out what he was going to wear. He had a big walk-in closet. One side was clothes that he always wore—his jeans and his shirts. The other side of the closet was where he kept his dress clothes that he only wore when he was forced to. He reached up and grabbed a pair of starched jeans and a starched white button-down shirt. This was a dance, after all, and in Texas starched anything was the perfect attire. He grabbed his dress Stetson, his best boots, and his belt. He was in such a rush he didn't really have time to think about how nervous he was about the dance. It had plagued him all week. But now, as he hurried down the stairs and saw Allie standing at the window in her beautiful dress with her hair cascading down her back and her pretty smile when she turned to look at him, he knew he was in trouble. Because all he was thinking about was dancing. And that was only an excuse for holding her.

And then there was the fact that he promised both of them that tonight they would pretend that they were really married. Which meant he very well might need to kiss her. And he wasn't sure he could do that. Not and keep his distance.

CHAPTER FOURTEEN

There were a lot of people at the wedding reception. Penny had a large ranch. Allie wasn't sure why she was surprised by this but she should've figured it out. Penny had been close to Wade's granddad and their ranches were very close to each other. There was oil all over Wade's family ranch, so she should've assumed that it would be the same way for Penny. But judging by all the different types of vehicles in the driveway, there was all manner of different financial situations for the people who were at the wedding reception. Which eased some of her discomfort a little bit. She wasn't going to be the only person here who wasn't used to money.

Wade helped her out of the truck and then looked at her. "Now tonight we're going to pretend that we met under normal circumstances and we got married and we're going to live happily ever after for the rest of our lives." There was a twinkle in his eyes as he said it. "Does that work for you? Does that make it okay for you tonight?"

He was doing this for her. And why in the world did it just feel so uncomfortable? But if she could pretend that they were actually in love, then maybe she could get through this. *Who was she kidding?* This was ridiculous. "Wade, there's no faking what we're doing. I just feel uncomfortable lying to everybody. I don't know what I was thinking when I said just pretending we were doing it would be okay. It's as wrong doing it that way as it is the other way."

To her surprise, he cupped her face between his hands. He smiled at her. "Allie, it's nobody's business but our own why we got married or when we will get unmarried. These people are here to be happy for us.

Let them be happy for us. You and I did what we needed to do and we have reasons for them to be happy for us. It may not be the exact reasons they are thinking but we can let them be happy. And I promised you I was going to give tonight my all, like if, well, you know, if we really had fallen in love and gotten married. So that's what I'm going to do. I figure if I don't do that, I'll be slighting you a little bit and I'm not going to do that. You helped me and my family out so much that I'm going to give you everything I can to make you feel comfortable and happy."

She could barely think straight with his hands cupping her face so gently and his eyes drilling into hers so sincerely. Her heart pounded and her mouth was getting drier by the moment, as if there were a dust storm going on in there. And if he had let go of her, she'd probably melt in a puddle because her knees had gone weak.

"You look startled. Are you scared?" His thumbs gently caressed her skin right in front of her ears. His fingertips splayed along her jawline and into her hairline.

She wanted so badly to turn her head so that she could feel his caress even better. "I'm not scared."

His eyes had mellowed and he nodded. "Good." And then to her complete and utter surprise, he lowered his lips to hers.

He was kissing her. And it felt so wonderful. It was magic. She was transported on cloud nine and sailed across a blue sky. Her knees got weaker. And to steady herself, her hands went to his waist and she held on. He didn't pull away and instead, when her mouth opened to his, he deepened the kiss. His hands left her face and moved to her shoulders and then pulled her close. And her hands that had been resting on his hips went around him and she held on tightly as she felt his body against hers. Felt his lips over hers.

"Okay, enough of that," he broke the kiss and muttered. Then came back for a quick peck on the lips. "Sorry. I got carried away." He laughed, almost nervously.

And she did too. "You sure know how to act."

"Yeah, I thought we needed to practice. You know, before we go in there and have to kiss—if we do."

"Sure, I understand." She would let him practice all he wanted.

Penny met them in the foyer. "Well, there you are." She winked at Allie. "Y'all ready to get this show started?"

Allie chuckled and looked up at Wade, thinking of the show he'd just put on outside for her. Allie had a feeling Penny would've been quite happy to witness that kiss. She was still reeling from it.

When they entered the back patio of the large house, people stood all across the patio and the lawn and the flagstone area surrounding a large pool. A refreshment area was set up over to the left and tables were scattered across the lawn with white tablecloths and flickering lights on them. Even though it was daylight still, she could see the flame in the candles. And there was a dance area set up: a large dance floor had been laid out and the band was softly playing.

"This is beautiful," she said, just as everyone erupted in cheers and claps and the band played an upbeat song.

The next twenty minutes were a muddled conglomeration in Allie's brain as she was introduced to so many people she knew she would never remember not a single name. This would be something she would learn over time, if she were going to be here for real and not just for three short months. She estimated a year and she would know everyone. But right now, she just let the names come in one side of her head and out the other because there was no way of retaining them.

Wade kept Allie's hand threaded through his arm as he introduced her to all the different people who had come to wish them well. His granddaddy had known and been liked by a lot of people, and Wade and his brothers had a lot of friends. He might not have had good luck where women were concerned, but he did have good friends.

And he was pretty much lying to all of them as he introduced her to one after the other. It rested full force on him why Allie had been so uncomfortable. He had played it down earlier as this was what his granddaddy had wanted. He didn't have any choice but now, face-to-face, telling all these good people that he and Allie were happily married, only to know that in less than two months they would be getting a divorce—it didn't sit well, lying to them like that. Allie had known this. It was his granddaddy's own fault. For about the hundredth time, he wondered what in the world his granddaddy had been thinking. Wade would probably go to his grave many years away from now, he hoped, still not understanding what his granddaddy was thinking.

This shindig was just like somebody had really gotten married. There was a huge, beautiful wedding cake. Allie had pretty much stopped breathing when she had seen it. And he had felt so bad for her. He hadn't known he could feel so bad.

Her hand on his arm had tightened so hard he thought she was going to draw blood. He tried to ignore it but he guessed every woman dreamed of a big wedding and a big wedding cake. And Penny had come through. He didn't know very much about wedding cakes, but if there was ever one that was ever any prettier than this one, he couldn't imagine it. And the beautiful table setting and the candlelight, and the band...yeah, Penny had gone all out, just like Granddaddy would have. Now she came up to them, smiling bigger than normal.

The first people he introduced her to were Todd and Morgan. They didn't look too happy but they were polite to Allie, and he could tell that they were surprised by her gentleness and genuineness.

"It's so nice to meet you." She seemed anxious when she looked from Todd to Morgan.

Beside her, he shot his brothers a look that he hoped told them they'd better behave. But he'd never believed they'd be unkind to her and they weren't.

"It's nice to meet you." Todd leaned in close. "And thanks for helping us out this way."

"I feel the same way. It's nice to meet you," Morgan said, sounding more cautious as he took her hand. He looked at Wade. "We need to talk later."

"Okay, you kiddos," Penny cut in. "It's time to cut that cake and after we cut the cake and get these festivities really going, you two are going to drink your wedding drink and take a bite of your wedding cake while the photographer takes your pretty pictures. And then we are going to play the wedding song and you two are going to go out there and dance together. I cannot wait. We're going to capture it all on camera and video."

She was taking photos like it was the real thing. He bet she even planned to have a wedding album. *And what was that for?*

"You do whatever you want to, Penny. I think Allie might be enjoying this?" He looked at her, hitching his eyebrow, just curious about what she would say.

"I'm a little overwhelmed. But I am enjoying it. I mean, to an extent. Thank you so much for throwing this party, Penny. You have really gone to a lot of trouble."

Penny chuckled and looked at her and then him and his brothers. "No trouble at all. It was my pleasure. As long as you two have a good time, that is all that matters. These boys' granddaddy and grandmother are probably getting a kick out of this right now. Now let's go cut some cake."

Wade grinned at her. "Shall we?" He crooked his arm and she slipped hers through his.

"She is wonderful," Allie said as they followed Penny to the cake.

"Yes, always has been."

Penny handed him a long, silver, fancy knife. He looked at it. And his face must've been blank because she laughed. "It's a cake-cutting knife for special occasions. I'm sure Allie knows this but I'll explain it to you, cowboy. You two both hold the handle of that and y'all slice a little piece of cake and then you feed her a piece and she feeds you a piece. You've been to enough weddings to know that, right?"

"Yes. Gotcha." He looked at Allie and she smiled at him.

"Please don't smush it in my face and I won't smush it in your face," she said softly.

A moment of mischief came over him and then he thought better of it. "I wouldn't do that to you." Not on a day like today, when their nerves were already rattled enough.

They stood behind the cake and the cameraman got across from them. Allie got up next to him and then he held the handle of the knife out to her and she placed her hand around it. He placed his hand on top of hers and felt her hand tremble beneath his. His mouth went dry. He got the sudden sensation of wondering what it would be like if this were real. She looked up at him and he looked at her. He wanted so much to give her...*give her what?* The real thing?

His brain went blank as he realized what was going on in there.

"Are we going to do this? You lead the way," Allie whispered, bringing him back to reality.

"Right. Okay, let's cut it now." He put pressure on the knife and they cut down one side of the cake and then lifted the knife out and cut along the other side and then someone handed him a plate. He slid the cake onto it. Allie actually led them on doing this; he just kept his hand wrapped tightly around hers. The cake ended up on the plate and everyone laughed.

"Okay, get a piece and you feed her and she'll feed you...just break a piece off there," Penny directed.

Allie got her piece and he got his piece, and then he looked at Allie. She watched him with so much vulnerability in her eyes, in the sweet expression that she wore, that his heart clenched. And then she held up the piece of cake that was in her hand and he realized that they needed to feed it to each other instead of him just standing there, gawking at her. Next thing he knew, he was biting into a piece of velvety vanilla cake and sweet creamy buttercream icing and she was too. Her mouth touched his hand and she giggled. He smiled big when he hadn't meant to push it in so hard and she had icing around her lips. Without thinking, he bent forward and kissed her lips, purposefully getting the icing off the side of her lips for her. She gasped and he whispered, "Supposed to be real." And then he kissed her again.

He heard the camera snapping and he heard the

people cheering. And he didn't care because Allie was kissing him back.

"That was wonderful," Penny exclaimed.

Allie was dazed and Penny's voice sounded as if it were coming at her from somewhere distant. Wade had kissed her twice. And he'd winked at her. And she felt as though she floated on air. This was dangerous—so, so dangerous. But it was supposed to be real, he had reminded her; it was all fake—they were just pretending like it was real. *They were pretending, they were pretending, they were pretending.*

"Okay, you two, the band's about to play. Let's go in that direction."

Allie looked at Penny and Penny winked at her. These winking people—she didn't know what to think of them. It was as if they were in on a joke that she wasn't in on.

Wade took her hand in his and they walked through the crowd that parted for them and out onto the dance floor. The band started playing something romantic. She was so out of it she couldn't even register what the song was, just that it was so beautiful, because Wade was with her. And then their bodies met as he wrapped an arm around her and held her other hand in his. They started dancing. They moved gently across the dance floor as he stared into her eyes and made her believe this was real. And then he spun her, letting go of one hand and then pulling her back to him, embracing as they moved to the music. She didn't know how to dance, and yet, she was dancing, moving with him as if they were born to move together. She laid her head on his shoulder. It was the easiest thing because it kind of hid her face from everybody. She knew the cameras were taking pictures and people were watching and she was trembling so bad she knew he could feel it too. *It was all a lie. It was all a lie.*

The words kept ringing in her ears as his heart beat against her temple and she wished with all her heart that this was real.

When the song ended, Wade whispered against her temple. "I guess we made believers out of them."

His words brought her back to the truth so quickly.

221

She looked at him. "Yes, I think we could both win an Oscar, don't you think?" The words were out of self-preservation. He couldn't know that her emotions were tangled together and that she had truly and deeply fallen in love with him.

She stepped away from him, smiling for everyone. But in her heart, she knew she had crossed the line somewhere and by the end of these three months, she was going to pay for that dearly.

The rest of the evening, they danced as much as possible. He realized, like her, that the more they danced together, the less they had to talk to anyone. At least she assumed that's what he realized because she realized it too. The rest of the time that they danced, she fought hard to not let her heart betray her any more deeply than it already had.

By the time they drove up to the house, she was tired and emotionally drained and ready to go to her room. She was so confused. In her heart of hearts, she wanted Wade to kiss her so badly. It was ridiculous. It was like she was a glutton for punishment. *What good could come from a kiss?* She remembered the moment he had kissed her when they were cutting the cake. It hadn't even been a deep kiss; it had just been a sweet, lingering kiss that she couldn't stop thinking about. And then there had been the kiss in the parking lot…

He opened the truck door for her and then took her hand to help her out of the truck. She walked across the concrete. She couldn't get inside quick enough to take off her shoes. Her heart hurt just as bad as her feet, and that was the kicker. They got inside the house. It had been a little bit awkward on the way home; they had talked briefly about the evening and about how Penny had pulled it off.

And that they had also pulled it off. *What a way to say it.* It's as if they had robbed a bank or pulled off a robbery. *A robbery of lies. A robbery of dreams.*

"Are you okay, Allie?" he asked quietly, standing there in the kitchen after they had walked through the garage entrance.

"Sure. How else am I supposed to be?"

"Well, you know, I was just making sure. I thought maybe you might be a little bit overwhelmed.

223

It was a big thing."

"Yes, it was. It was beautiful."

"Yes, it was." They stared at each other and then he took a step toward her. "We did well, though. We told them what they wanted to hear and I hope I held up my end of the bargain."

Her heart thundered. She told herself to turn and go to her room now. Nothing good could come of this. "You did."

He took another step toward her. Then his hands were dipped into her hair and he stared down at her as he held her face in his hands. "You were so beautiful tonight. And everyone loved you."

What was she supposed to say to that? She swallowed hard and didn't say anything. She didn't know what to say. *Could he hear her heart thundering?*

And then he bent his head and he kissed her. The next thing she knew, her arms were around him again and they were kissing. When he suddenly broke the kiss and stepped back from her, she regretfully let him go. She had known that's what would happen. Known he would come to reality. She was prepared.

"Goodnight, Wade." She turned and hurried through the kitchen door into the living space to the hallway, to the landing, up the stairs, down the hall and through her door, closing it quickly behind her. She never looked back.

CHAPTER FIFTEEN

Wade rode out early the next morning to work with the men.

She was glad for the space and used it to call Ginny.

"Ginny, can you get away and come spend a couple of days with me?" Allie clutched the phone between her hands as she stared out the window of her bedroom.

"What's wrong? You sound very upset." Ginny was tapping her fingernails on the table and Allie could hear it over the phone. Ginny did that when she was getting upset or angry.

Allie tried to control the tremor in her voice. She'd barely slept all night, reliving the moments of Wade kissing her. And the moments that they'd shared, smiling and hugging and pretending at the wedding reception. *How had she let herself, in those few hours, fall into a rabbit hole of believing that this was possible?* "I'm fine. It's just hit me that I'm in over my head."

"I knew you were going to get hurt."

"I know you did. But Ginny, he's wonderful. I didn't really understand how wonderful."

Ginny growled on the other end of the line. "And Mr. Wonderful is going to break my girl's heart. Allie, listen to me—pull back, right now. Don't let your heart get involved any more. That cowboy told you clearly this would be for three months and then he was going to walk away. I just knew when I saw that look in your eye last week that this was happening."

Allie could see Ginny about to have a fit on the other end of the line. She was probably up pacing now because her fingers were no longer tapping on the table. She'd invited Ginny in hopes that she would be able to come to the wedding reception, but Ginny hadn't been able to get away. She was heavily involved in the boutique winery her parents owned. Ginny loved the vineyard. She worked hard growing those grapes to perfection and making their Texas wine the best it could be. They had a very good reputation. "I know you said you couldn't get away for the party last night but this week maybe? They're getting Mama settled later this week but I could really use you to hang out with this week."

"Nope. I'm packing as we speak. My business can wait a day. Besides, Dad's been a little weird lately and he's driving me crazy. I think I need a break from him. I'm not sure what has gotten into him. He's going over the books with a fine-tooth comb. Double-checking my work is not something I like or appreciate. Even if it is his business for now. But this is about you, and I need to come pay this cowboy billionaire, Mr. Moneybags, a visit. And pull you off the ledge. There hasn't been any…"

"No. But he kissed me. And I kissed him. And

Ginny, it was magical. I've never ever felt anything like it before. It's like there's a connection."

"Stop. Stop it right now. There's no connection— *no* connection. There's a disconnection in less than two months now, remember? Disconnect. Disconnect."

Allie dropped her forehead to her palm and stared at the table. "Yes, you're right. I know, I know. But I'm in trouble, Ginny. I need you to come help me get my heart lassoed and stuffed back in that iron pen so it can't get out again."

"Well, you just hang on. I'm on my way. Text me the address and I'll plug it into my GPS. I'll get there about as fast as I can drive. Daddy will understand. I think he will be relieved, actually."

"I love you, Ginny. Ginny to my rescue, as always." She wished she hadn't had to say that. Ginny had always told her she was too vulnerable and she was. It was just so aggravating she wanted to kick something, but she would probably just break her toe if she did. "I can't wait to see you."

After they hung up, she sent the address and looked at the time. It would be late, maybe even dark before she got here. She was so glad Nelda wasn't around and that Wade hadn't made it in from working yet either. She hadn't needed to run into him today. She needed space.

Space to get back on track and find her way back from the ledge, as Ginny so accurately called the edge of disaster she was balanced on so precariously.

It was late in the afternoon when Wade finally got up the nerve to go back home. He was tired and dusty, having ridden out to work fence with some of his men. Nothing better than digging post holes to make a guy forget something he wished he hadn't done and give him time to think about it and what he could do about it. The blazing hot sun had beat down on him and he was sweating like a hog. He smelled awful by the time he strode into the kitchen. Being so dirty would be a good excuse not to linger when he ran into Allie. He was walking through the living room when he spotted her sitting over in the corner with a book in her hand, looking out the window.

She would've been able to see him riding up. He paused; he yanked his dusty hat off his head and held it between his hands. His heart had kicked up when she looked at him. And Lord help him, he wanted to stride across that room and pull her up out of that seat and kiss her.

He was in so much stinking trouble.

How had this happened? "I had to go work fence this morning. Are you doing okay?"

She closed the book and nodded.

He felt guilty because he knew she knew he was using an excuse. *Since when did he turn into a coward?*

"I hope you got the fence built really well. Looked like you worked hard enough."

"Yeah, we did."

"Um, I think we need to talk." She stood.

"You're probably right. Look, about last night. I probably shouldn't have kissed you like that."

"No, don't apologize. I'm the one who goaded you into pretending that this was a real marriage. And that's all you were doing. And I don't

231

know…somewhere along the way, maybe we got carried away. But I just need you to know that I understand that nothing else is going to come of that. There's no need for you to feel awkward. I know nothing has changed. Don't worry."

He opened his mouth to deny what she was saying, that he wasn't worried about it and that he hadn't been pretending. But that would not do. He had gotten so mixed up and he wasn't a man who got mixed up very often. His granddaddy taught him that. *"You make your mind up about what you want and you go get it. But be a man of your word."* That was how he lived until now and he had said at three months, it was done and he'd walk away. They were in this for only one reason, and yet, he really wasn't sure he could walk away—or whether he wanted to walk away.

But could he change his mind? He halted his thoughts. "We'll get this figured out. But I understand that it was just pretend."

She nodded. "I mean, you know, I'm getting what I wanted and my mother is getting the best care. I guess at the end of the three months, I got plans. I'm going to go on—I'm going to open my florist shop again as soon as Mama is out of the coma and I get her out of the rehab center and back home recuperating."

"Oh, that sounds good."

"Yes, thanks to our agreement. I've invited Ginny down for a few days. She'll be here in the next hour. I hope you don't mind. I just wanted to warn you. We're going to spend some time tomorrow looking at the ranch. And I think it will be good. We will go and check out the rehab center where they'll be bringing my mother also."

Both relief and dread filled him. It would be good for her to have her friend here and take some pressure off both of them. And he also knew he was going to get an earful from Ginny. Ginny was going to remind him of exactly what he had forgotten last night. And she was probably bringing Loretta to remind him how vulnerable Allie could be. After all, she was still mourning the death of her daddy, and then there was her mother.

"I'm glad she's coming." Allie obviously needed

to see her. "I'll do whatever I can to help y'all have a good visit. Is she going to stay a few days? She's very welcome to stay as long as she wants."

"She's going to stay for just probably a couple days. I don't think she can stay away from their boutique winery for too long."

He laughed. She was really cute when she got flustered. "While she's here, we should drive over and let me show y'all our vineyard. Todd runs the business. We make grape jelly and wine. Ginny's been in the wine business for a long time?"

"Yes, she has, and she loves it. She lives and breathes grapes."

"I'm surprised that she does this."

"She loves it and she will love visiting yours. And I know that you don't get along with her well, so thank you for being so understanding."

"I don't dislike Ginny. I barely know her. But what I do know is you love her and she is in your corner one hundred percent. And I like that about her. She's looking out for you."

"Wade, I don't mind telling you I get irritated

sometimes about everyone looking out for me. I am a grown woman. She's my friend and I need her support as a friend but I can look out for myself. Yes, I am a little bit vulnerable—she keeps drilling that into me. I mean, I have been through a lot this last little while but I'm managing." Her voice broke and she struggled; he could see her struggling.

His heart ached for her. He'd been there once when his own parents had died. And plus, instead of helping her, he'd added to her stress last night. "I remember what you're going through. I was younger than you when I lost my mom and dad, and my granddaddy was still making decisions for me back then, so I had my grief. But I didn't have a whole world of decisions to make sitting on my shoulders. And though Granddaddy died four months ago, it's different. You're helping me with that so I'll survive, but that's not the kind of pressure that you're under. Even if I had lost this ranch, I wouldn't have been devastated financially. You have been so strong, trying to deal with everything on your own. The grief, the worry about your mama, working yourself to the bone just trying to stay afloat. And then you having lost your own business on top of that. Nope, what we have been going through doesn't compare to each other. It's going to get better for you, and I hope that what we've done will help. But I feel like I took advantage of you last night."

"No, you didn't." She took a few steps toward him.

He held up his hand. "You probably don't want to get too close to me. I've sweated—it was hot out there today."

Her smile surprised him and joy bloomed inside him just looking at her. "I'm going to go take a shower. But I'm glad your friend's coming. And I'll do whatever I can to help you have a good time. But you rest easy. We've got that wedding reception thing behind us and we're going to go back to putting some space between us. I won't be kissing you like that again, so rest easy."

She nodded and he thought she looked sad.

Then she took a step back. "I think you're right."

He paused at the base of the steps. "I'm going to

go work in my office after dinner."

"Okay then. I made some King Ranch Chicken. It's warming in the oven."

"Sounds good."

"Just get what you want. I'm going to read in my room until Ginny gets here."

"Okay." They sounded like strangers. He didn't like it but turned and walked away. He had never felt so awkward in his life. *How could a few kisses change everything?*

After his shower, Wade went to his office. He hadn't been in there but five minutes when Morgan called him.

"How's it going with you and Allie?"

Morgan sounded as though he were in the air. Morgan lived a much more high-profile life than Wade did, or wanted to. Running the hotels like he did, his life was filled with meetings and planning sessions that required a lot more travel than Wade's.

"Are you heading somewhere?"

"Yeah. I'm on the way to a black-tie event at the California hotel. You got the invitation, which I'm sure you ignored like you ignore most of them."

"You and I both know that is not something that I have to be at. The hotel chain and resorts are your passion."

"Yeah, but our shareholders don't mind seeing you there sometimes too."

"Well, they're just going to hold their breath for right now. I've got things on my mind that don't include schmoozing with them." It irritated him to have people think he was at their beck and call. That was probably the one thing about the hotel chain side of their money—the people involved, they had a lot of people counting on them for their jobs. Thankfully, Morgan didn't mind. He enjoyed it, actually. There was something about that side of the life that challenged Morgan and so for that, Wade was grateful. Saved him having to pretend that he liked dressing up in a tuxedo or a suit. Nope—give him his Wranglers and his ropers and he was just fine.

And Allie.

The thought hit him like cold water.

Morgan asked a question and he heard it at a distance.

"You didn't answer my question. How are you and your bride doing?" Morgan asked again.

Wade shook off the thought of Allie smiling and kissing him. "We're doing all right. Thanks for being kind last night." *Could he tell his brother what he was feeling?*

"She did seem like she was sweet. Like she could get hurt. Wade, I watched her all night and that woman is into you."

He hung his head. He pulled himself together. "She is sweet. And we have an agreement. We were acting like it was real last night. That's all."

"Right. Look, Wade, you looked happy last night. If this lady is everything she looked like last night and everything you swear she is, then why are you going to let her go at the end of three months?"

"Because that is what we agreed to."

"But can't agreements be broken?"

"It's not that easy. Allie is known for being vulnerable and right now with her life so torn up, even more so. I can't take advantage of that. How am I supposed to know she's thinking straight?"

"Does that mean your perspective on marriage has changed?"

Had it? "She might have changed the tide some. I know there are good women out there. At least, she is."

Morgan was silent. "Sounds really complicated. I've got a bad feeling that Granddaddy's going to do something with the hotels. And if he's going to tell me that I have to get married or lose the hotels, I don't know what I'll do. I'm just warning you now that I'm looking at options. Because I'm not sure I'll jump through his hoops."

"Morgan, you and I both know that the hotels have investors. It wouldn't be so easy to do this to you, would it? It could put the shareholders in jeopardy. He may have gotten more creative on you. I can't come up with what but he's got something weird up his sleeve."

"I hope you're right," he said, strain in his voice.

"I just can't get over what he did. Or the fact that you actually went through with it. Look, I was pretty rough on you when you first told us. Well, thank you for doing what you're doing. I might not be at the ranch that often but I didn't want to lose it either. So I owe you. If I can do anything to help you, let me know."

That meant a lot to Wade. "Thanks. If I need anything, I'll let you know. And Morgan, thanks for calling."

CHAPTER SIXTEEN

Ginny arrived in record time. She pulled into the ranch driveway just after dark and Allie was waiting on the porch.

"I am so glad to see you." Allie called, as she hurried across the yard toward her friend. They had spoken several times during the day but seeing her burst from the Jeep grinning made Allie almost tear up.

"Allie girl!" Ginny yelled and ran toward Allie. She had on her boots with her jeans tucked in and her cowboy hat that had crinkles all over it. There was a big feather on the front of it, with some kind of jewel that shined in the porch light.

They hugged and jumped around a little bit. Despite seeing each other briefly last week on her trip back to Tyler, it had been more subdued in the room with her mother, where quietness was a must.

"I am so glad you came to see me."

"I had to come kick your rear into gear."

They both giggled.

"I need you to."

Ginny gave her a *I'm-here-for-you* look. "Be prepared. Tomorrow I'm probably going to get me a piece of that husband of yours. He's got your mind spinning and I'm here to stop that merry-go-round."

Arm in arm, they walked back to the house and into the kitchen as they talked.

"I was freaking out when I called you, but I've calmed down. I didn't tell you I'd calmed down on the phone because I didn't want you to turn around and go home. I still wanted you to come see me. But he's not completely to blame here, you know. I urged him to let the dance be real. I just wasn't prepared for what real meant for me and my fickle little heart."

"There is not one thing wrong with your heart. It is the *best* heart I've ever known or ever will know. It is not fickle. It is loyal, and wonderful and gentle and passionate. And men are fools for not seeing that. You are going to have a fabulous family one day when the man of your dreams sweeps you off your feet and treats you like the gem you are. You will have all those children you long for, the ones you've wanted all your life. And these sweet-talking or slick-talking cowboys without a dollar to their name who steal your money and try to make you think you are less than you are can go jump in a lake."

Allie's heart grabbed. The pain of what a fool she'd been months ago pained her.

"And it won't be from this handsome money-bags cowboy either. He's using you, just like the others."

"No, no—he helped me, too. *They* didn't."

"True. But he's not the one. Don't let his helping you mix up your feelings for this guy. You are both helping each other out, so please do not forget that. I'm going to remind you every day I'm here and every day after I leave if I need to. But before I leave, he'll know to back off and let you have your space. I brought Loretta and I'm going to let him know I did."

Allie groaned. "No, you didn't. There is not going to be any need for you to whip that thing out to scare him."

Ginny grinned. "You know I travel everywhere with Loretta. But he doesn't need to know that. He's going to think, unless you tell him, that I carried it over here just for him. Stick with me and we'll get him in order."

Allie had to laugh as she stared at her friend. Pure Texas country girl full of mischief and determination. Allie loved Ginny, but poor, poor Wade. *What had she done?*

Wade woke at his normal five-thirty in the morning and went down to the barn, using his balcony door as his exit instead of chancing waking Allie and Ginny. He had overheard their conversation the night before. He'd been going to welcome her and been in the hallway when he'd overheard Allie say she had a fickle heart. He'd halted as Ginny's forceful words hit him. *"There is not one thing wrong with your heart. It is the best heart I've ever known or ever will know. It is not fickle. It is loyal, and wonderful and gentle and passionate. And men are fools for not seeing that."* He hadn't been able to move but had stood there as they talked about him and other men who had hurt Allie. *What?* Someone had stolen from her? Used her? Made her feel like she was *less than*?

Ginny's description did not sit well with him. Allie was good and loyal and kind and giving and every good description he could come up with but in no way was she less than anything or anyone. So when he'd met her, she hadn't just been grieving her dad and worried about her mother; she had been mistreated and used. He wanted to ask who these men were and he wanted to stand up for Allie, and to get back what had been hers. But he also wanted to make her know that she was everything and more than Ginny had said she was.

And he wanted to walk in there and give Ginny a big hug and a kiss on the cheek for bringing this to his attention.

He wanted to make this right.

Allie had taken up for him and he knew in his heart that he wasn't in the same category as those other cowboys. He would never have intentionally hurt her.

But what next?

He'd moved back from the door and gone to his room for the night to think. This morning, he was completely winging it, prepared for Ginny to blast him but determined to make this right if he could. About eight, after clearing the day for himself, he walked back up to the house and found them sitting outside on the back deck, eating breakfast. They'd made cinnamon buns. His stomach growled.

"Morning, ladies." He gave Ginny a nod of his head and tipped his hat. Allie looked tired. But at least this morning there was a twinkle back in her eye that hadn't been there the day before.

Ginny hiked a brow. "Morning yourself, cowboy." Ginny gave him an unexpected smile.

"I hope you had a good drive down, Ginny."

"I did and I dreamed all the way down here all the

different things I was going to do to you when I got here. You are treading on thin ice, bucko."

"Ginny, please," Allie said, pleading in her voice. "We talked about this."

"Allie doesn't want me to say anything to you. But she was upset when she called me and asked me to come visit. I'm here because I think you might be playing with her heart."

The woman did not mince words.

Allie had turned beet-red. "Ginny, we talked about this last night. I told you not to say anything. Wade and I will work this out."

Wade took his hat off so Allie could see his eyes. "No, Ginny's right, Allie. I should've told you the other day when you said we would treat the dance like it was real—I should've put my foot down right there and said no. That if you couldn't fake it at the dance then we shouldn't do it. I should've just told Penny we didn't need a wedding reception. I don't know what I was thinking."

"It's okay, Wade."

"No, it's not okay. We signed a contract. We have

it written out and I let myself deviate from it. And I'm making a promise to you both that it won't happen again. We can be friends but we're not crossing that line again. We have about eight weeks to go now and I let us get off track. Ginny is just here to remind me of what is at stake here. Ginny, you're not going to have to get that gun out."

Ginny smiled but it didn't reach her eyes. They were very steady on his. "I think that sounds just dandy. The contract you signed was cut-and-dried. And I think that's the way it needs to stay. 'Course, that's just me. If Allie tells me she fell head over heels in love with you, then we would have to have another talk."

This Ginny was something. *What? Was she going to get out her shotgun and have a shotgun wedding when they were already married?* It didn't quite make sense. But again, at least she was looking out for Allie. "I give you my word, friends is all we're going to be. I won't cross the line again."

Allie bit her lip and he feared he saw disappointment in her eyes. *Not good.*

Ginny slid the plate of cinnamon rolls toward him. "Great. Now I can relax and we can have some fun. Want a cinnamon roll?"

Relief should have filled him but he didn't feel anything but anxious as he reached for the cinnamon roll. "Thanks. Can't resist these." He was afraid he was going to have trouble resisting Allie but he would. "Would you two like to go visit our vineyard? See where we make our jelly and our wine?"

Both ladies smiled and said yes in unison. And he at least felt as if he were doing something right.

Allie looked from Wade to Ginny and felt some relief that they called a truce of sorts. She had mixed feelings about Wade so firmly assuring Ginny that the next eight weeks would be strictly by the contract. But at least for now she was on firmer ground. This was good.

She wasn't sure why she needed Ginny to like Wade. After all, in eight weeks it wouldn't matter. They probably wouldn't ever run into each other after the marriage was dissolved. Them meeting on that fateful night at the truck stop had been a once-in-a-million chance.

Wade took a bite of the cinnamon roll. "Amazing. I'm going to go get a cup of coffee and do a few things in the office. When y'all are ready, you let me know."

Allie took a sip of her coffee. "How about an hour? Ginny and I are going to have a little bit more of this coffee first. We were up late last night."

"Yes, sounds good." Allie met his gaze and his chest felt as though it were on fire.

Ginny held her arms over her head and stretched. "I have to say, this is a beautiful house and that bed in the room I'm in is about as comfortable of a bed as I've ever slept in. I honestly can't believe you live in this big house all by yourself normally."

"I didn't use to live in it by myself. It was my granddaddy's and I lived here because I didn't want him rambling around in it alone. But through the years there's been more of us here. Todd and Morgan lived here too at one point before they took over their parts of the business. It's been filled. And then when

Morgan got married, he and his wife would visit."

Allie stared at him. "Morgan used to be married? You've not mentioned that."

He looked sad. "He was married. But we don't talk about it much. He doesn't want to and we do what he asked. He lost his wife. She got sick about three years ago. So I guess Granddaddy figured that was the end of his chance of getting any great-grandkids. And the reality is he did because he died too, before any of us fulfilled his dream. A dream I hadn't realized he wanted so badly until he pulled this stunt with his will."

Wade looked out toward the fields for a minute, a very thoughtful expression on his face. Then he looked back at her.

"I never quite thought about it from my granddaddy's perspective on him and this ranch and how much life there used to be here when we were all kids growing up and getting into stuff. It was lively, and a lot of laughter. There hasn't been laughter here in a long time. I think he wanted that back."

"I'm so sorry. But I guess you're thinking he was

really sad about that. About it being so quiet."

"Yeah. I mean, he hinted at us getting married but he never really pushed. And you know, for him that was odd. Usually if he wanted something, he made it happen."

Allie studied him. She could see that he was disturbed. Her gaze shifted to Ginny and she actually saw something flicker in her friend's eyes that looked like compassion. Allie wanted to comfort him but she pulled her emotions back. There would be none of that.

Ginny spoke up. "I'm thinking he realized he couldn't make y'all fall in love but then decided what the heck and decided to try anyway. Sometimes you have to shake things up to make things happen."

Wade and Ginny stared at each other and Allie wondered what they were thinking.

"Maybe so," Wade said. "Well, it's coffee time. I'll see you two in an hour." With that, he turned and strode into the house.

Ginny looked across the table at Allie. "He just seems lonesome to me."

Allie agreed. "Yes, he does. And I have a feeling

that his granddaddy probably was too. I can just feel how badly he wanted great-grandkids. I mean, this place is just so beautiful and for him to know that if all his boys weren't interested in getting married, it was always going to be quiet... Can you imagine how that felt for him, building this place up and having seen how lively it had been with boys running around and enjoying this land so much and then to suddenly not see any of that? I think you're right. I think he was desperate when he made that will. And I think he did what he did out of love."

Ginny shrugged and took a sip of her coffee. "I get what you're saying. I didn't know the guy but heck, you know how my mom and dad are about wanting me to get married and give them grandbabies to run around in the vineyard. They keep saying they want to hear the laughter of children running through those grapevines. I used to play in that dirt growing up. It's a great life. But I told them that they were just going to have to hold their horses because it was probably going to be awhile before I thought about hitching myself to a man."

"When the time is right, you'll find the right guy and he's going to love you for yourself. Just like you are always telling me."

"Right." She held her coffee mug up and nodded toward Allie. Allie lifted her coffee cup and they clinked them together. "To you and me, Allie. May we find the lives we want and the loves in our time. And the right loves—on our terms."

Allie giggled. "You always want everything on your terms."

Ginny grinned. "Is there any other way? I mean, why not?"

"You're right. Why settle?"

"Absolutely no reason to settle. Now let's talk about what you're going to do over the next eight weeks while you're here being friends with your fake husband."

"I hate to break it to you but right now he's not a fake husband. He's my real husband."

Her entire forehead wrinkled above her glare.

"You didn't make it real, real. Right?"

Allie's cheeks heated. "No, we have not."

"Whew! I'm glad to know that. I thought I really might have gotten here too late."

Allie took a sip of her coffee and hoped that hid the emotions that raced through her just at the thought of sharing any kind of intimacy with Wade. There would be no way of salvaging her heart.

CHAPTER SEVENTEEN

Wade took them through the arched entrance that said McCoy Stonewall Jelly and Wine Division. He felt a sense of pride at the beautiful rows of grapes that reached as far as you could see. The house sat in the distance, a large place with a Tuscan look and a second-floor wraparound upper balcony that enabled a view of the vines.

This was Todd's pride and passion. Wade enjoyed the jelly but had personally never been a lover of wine. The grape jelly had come first, years ago, but then his granddaddy had expanded into wine after he bought more acreage and saw the potential. He'd also realized Todd understood the vision. His granddaddy was good at matching people with their passions.

"This is some place," Ginny said from the backseat.

"It is beautiful," Allie agreed.

"Todd has built this into what it is."

"McCoy Stonewall wines are good," Ginny added.

When they stopped at the house, she got out and headed straight to the vines. Felt them, looked at them, and bent down and dug her fingers in the dirt, letting it sift through her fingertips back to the ground as she studied it.

Wade and Allie saw Todd approaching and waved.

He did the same as he walked up. "Hey, about time Wade brought you to see the place. We'll give you the tour if you have time."

"Your place is gorgeous," Allie said, as Ginny walked over. "This is my best friend, Ginny. Ginny, this is Todd, Wade's brother."

"Nice to meet you." Todd held out his hand.

Ginny dusted her hand off on her thigh then took his hand and Allie could have sworn she flushed slightly beneath her well-tanned skin. She was outside working with her vines all day and always had sun-bronzed skin which acted as camouflage for the suspected blush.

"Nice to meet you too," she said, her brow creased. "You know, you need to prune your vines back more. It would raise your sun exposure."

Todd's brow creased to match Ginny's as he released her hand and looked at his vines and then back at Ginny. "My vines are perfectly pruned. I do much of it myself."

"Well, you're doing a poor job. I'm telling you, this crop could increase with a little better sun exposure. And your wine depth would be—"

"Excuse me—what do you know about wine?"

"Ginny's family has a winery in Tyler. The Rossi Rose of Tyler Vineyard." Allie didn't like the look on Ginny's face. Ginny was passionate about the growth and care of a grape. Something Allie knew very little about but her friend was obsessed with making the best wine Texas had ever seen. She believed at her small family-owned winery she could make it happen.

"It's a small boutique winery, but excellent," Ginny added, tartly. "I prune my vines too."

"Good for you," Todd said. "I won't tell you how to do it." He looked at Wade. "Maybe we better do the tour. Do you want to see the jelly facility first?"

"No, the vines. Jelly is jelly," Ginny responded instantly, before Wade could reply.

Wade glanced at Allie, wondering what was up with her friend. Allie looked worried. Wade returned his attention on Todd and Ginny.

Todd was staring at her, his expression a mixture of a man fighting for patience and fighting to be polite. "Our Stonewall Jelly is a work of art."

She laughed. "Wine is a work of art. Jelly just takes a few grapes, a heap of sugar, and some fire. Wine takes so much more. Surely you're not wasting these quality grapes on jelly?"

Wade looked at Allie again and she cringed and mouthed, "Sorry." He gave an imperceptible shrug.

Todd, on the other hand, laughed. But there was

no humor in his laugh. "Our mainstay of this business is our jelly. That's where our history is. I do have a passion for the winemaking and although it is growing and making waves in the industry, it's our McCoy's Stonewall Jelly that is our superpower so yes, we are, as you say, wasting some of our grapes on jelly. More than half actually."

She shook her head. "That's just sad. But I'd love to see your process with the wine."

"Jelly is very important to our business." Todd's jaw tightened then looked at Wade and Allie with a who-does-she-think-she-is expression. "Y'all come this way. We're going to check out my wine-making process." Then he turned and strode toward the building she assumed held the wine.

Allie spent the next hour in turmoil as Ginny and Todd argued over "processes" and Wade looked on, with his lips twitching a lot watching his brother and her friend. Todd wasn't smiling, instead his eyes flashed fire nearly every time Ginny spoke.

By the time they left, she felt as if Ginny had insulted Todd in every way possible.

When they got back to the ranch, Wade suggested that maybe they might like to take a truck and explore the ranch. Or go lunch somewhere and not have him tag along. Allie wasn't fooled; he was ready to escape.

"We're going to head to the rehab and check it out. We'll eat somewhere on the way. And might eat dinner on the way back." She needed space from him and time to let Ginny chill. Her friend seemed really wound up after the time spent at the winery.

The minute they were in the truck and heading toward Kerrville, where they'd finally decided was the best place for her mother and not as far away as San Antonio from the ranch, she glanced at Ginny. "What was up with you torturing Todd?"

Ginny crossed her arms and frowned. "It just irks me that he has all of that amazing space to do with as he wants, and yet, the man refuses to listen to good advice. He took one look at me and dismissed everything I said."

It was true. He had. It was as if the two of them had no common ground. It had been painful to watch and also, interesting. Allie thought she might have seen a spark between them.

"You were pretty hard on him."

"I told him the truth. Arrogant…maybe it's the money."

"Maybe, but I don't think so. You never told him your label. I'm sure—"

"Nope, the man is a wine snob. Wine from Tyler, in his book, is secondary. Besides, he never asked. He assumed I was some home winemaker."

"He's really handsome, don't you think?"

"Yes, and he knows it."

"Were you attracted to him?"

"Ha. Now you, my friend, are delusional. Nope. And don't try getting this visit on me and my nonexistent love life. I'm not ready for all that. Whereas you, my friend, are totally ready. I have been thinking about this. I think part of why you are so mixed up about Wade is that you are so ready for that family you want. I'm thinking when you get home, maybe we can set you up on a dating app. That way we can really vet the guys before you meet them."

Allie started to protest then stopped. "That might

actually be a good idea. But we need to wait until Mama comes through this coma. I just can't go through the stress of that and dating. With what Wade has done for me with the money and care she is getting, I'm going to open my florist shop back up and concentrate on that and Mama for a while. And there will be no men in my future until then." She meant it, too. It was time to stand on her own and this gift that was Wade and his crazy marriage deal was her second chance at life. Not love. And she would keep that in mind.

Two days later, when Ginny gave her a hug and then drove away, she and Allie both were feeling more confident that she could do this without coming out heartbroken.

She had decided to go ahead and start planning her florist shop and to use her extra time to get everything she could set up from here. She'd find a place, and she realized that she wasn't held to Tyler; she could open anywhere. And taking to heart her need to stand on her own feet, she decided to look for the perfect place with the best opportunity for success.

She had a plan and she was determined to stick to it.

And she would not let her heart out of the cage she'd rebuilt around it.

The next weeks of her life on the ranch were a bit strained. Nelda came back to work and her mother was doing great. Her own mother was transferred to the rehab unit and she started spending time there at least every other day. She was so grateful to Wade for having spent the money to have her transferred. Wade had gone with her to visit one day and they'd stopped for dinner at a place in Fredericksburg. It was a nice place with outdoor dining and it had been in many ways romantic. She had fought off any emotions that had her longing for him to let down the new wall that he'd put up between them. She knew it was for the best and got on herself for even thinking about getting past that barrier.

After that night, he seemed to put up the barrier even more and he seemed to have more out-of-town cattle buying trips and late evenings working with his cowboys.

And she spent longer days with her mother and when she wasn't, she was doing research on where she wanted to open her business. She kept looking in areas that were far too close to Stonewall for her own good and had finally settled on College Station. It was a vibrant, growing town with many opportunities and not too terribly far from Tyler. She or Ginny could sneak away for weekends if they wanted to. And there was a regional airport if she needed that.

Her plan was coming together. The only thing that wasn't was this longing she hadn't quite been able to overcome that she and Wade might have met under different circumstances and that he might have fallen in love with her. But that was just a dream. The other thing that was holding her back was that her mother wasn't improving and she looked paler. She left, not feeling comfortable about going home but assured by the nurses that they would contact her if anything changed. She was nearing the ranch when the nurse called and said her mother was in danger of developing pneumonia.

Pneumonia. Her heart lurched. Her hands trembled as she drove up the drive to the ranch. She stopped before she reached the garage and looked across at the stables.

Wade was in the riding pen. Every ounce of her being longed to feel his arms around her. She'd been feeling that and fighting it for weeks now, refusing to cross that line that they'd made when Ginny had been here to visit. But right then, she felt weak and needed him. Not stopping to think, she got out of the car and walked across the lot. She watched him and her heart thrummed with need and a longing so overpowering that she couldn't resist it.

He was a wonderful rider and she'd learned that part of his passion was training horses. She missed sitting with him on the porch and talking. Those talks had disappeared right after he had promised her that he wouldn't cross the line again. They had spent as little time as possible together, although when they were around each other they were cordial and polite and oh so distant and constrained. Even Nelda had started to pick up on tension between them.

Thankfully, Nelda was discreet enough not to ask Allie whether they were having problems. But Allie knew that the housekeeper had picked up on the fact that they were not sleeping in the same room and had said nothing. But Allie could see concern in her eyes.

Allie had known it was only a matter of time before the separate bedroom ruse exploded on them. But she didn't have any worry that Nelda would say anything to hurt them. Or, if, in fact, anyone cared anyway. She had a feeling Wade's granddaddy had just concocted a way to get his soured-on-women-and-love grandson to give it one more shot. She didn't think he had set up spies on him. That, she believed, he would have thought was going too far. At least she wanted to believe that was how he felt.

She stopped at the fence and watched him. He glanced at her and her heart lunged against the barriers and nearly knocked the breath out of her. His gaze was raw and she saw longing there, too, before he snapped down the shutters and closed her out. *Did he care for her like she cared for him?* This contract had become an unsurmountable mountain between them.

"Wade." She said his name ever so softly.

He turned his horse and rode toward her. "What's wrong? Weren't you visiting your mom?"

She didn't bother to tell him she had been with her mother. It hit her that he could tell something was wrong by just looking at her. "She's having some issues that are scaring me. The doctors said they're watching her close but that she is in danger of getting pneumonia."

He dismounted. "That's not good. Has she been having trouble?"

"The last few days she's been having some issues. Small things."

"And you didn't tell me." His eyes shadowed and she felt bad.

"I didn't want to bother you—"

He reached through the iron bars of the pen and cupped her bicep. "Allie, you are not a bother." His gaze was piercing and then he looked away—let his hand drop away, too—and she felt his frustration.

She wasn't sure what she was seeing, though. She

felt like a bother to him. That he was impatient for the end of the three months so he could get back to his life and his ranch and not worry about her being around anymore.

"Look, let me put the horse in the shade and then we can talk."

"I would like that," she said, really needing to talk to him. She knew she could call Ginny but she knew all the way home from the rehab center that she wanted to talk to Wade.

"I'll be out of this fence in just a minute. Don't go anywhere."

She wasn't planning on it. At least not for now.

Wade couldn't believe Allie hadn't told him her mother had taken a turn for the worse. He had been struggling with staying away from her. And it was driving him crazy. All he thought about was Allie. His concentration was suffering and he was starting to feel as if the date they were supposed to dissolve the marriage was going to be the worst day of his life.

He wanted to talk to her, to know about her day and to tell her about his day. And he'd been holding back because he thought that was what she wanted.

And her not telling him something as important as news about her mother hurt.

She was waiting where he left her. His heart ached seeing the worry in her eyes. He wanted to take her into his arms and hold her and tell her that everything was going to be all right. But he knew that all the money in the world couldn't help some things. And where her mother was concerned, he'd done everything that could be done and all he could do now was give support and comfort to Allie. And to pray that her mother would be okay and hopefully open her eyes soon.

"Let's go back and check on her. I'll take you there right now and we'll stay as long as needed. Pack an overnight bag if you want and we'll get a hotel close to the rehabilitation center so you'll be closer. Whatever you need, I'll do it. All you need to do is ask."

She stared at him with those big eyes that looked

huge and lost. It was all he could do not to reach for her.

"Could you hold me for a minute?"

"*H-hold* you?" He couldn't believe she wanted him to hold her. "Yes, sure, if that's what you want." He strode to her and gently took her in his arms. She smelled of sweetness and sunshine and everything nice in his world. His heart thundered as he pulled her closer. He closed his eyes and breathed her in and had to restrain from holding her too tightly because his every instinct was driving him to hold her and never let her go.

"Thank you," she said, so softly he had to dip his head to hers to hear her words.

"I'm here for you, darlin'."

"They told me that she could turn for the worse or the better at any time. Wade, I haven't let myself think about the possibility of her not coming out of this coma." She lifted her head so she could look up at him. "The moment they told me, all I could think about was telling you and letting you reassure me that it was going to be okay."

He closed his eyes, knowing that was the one thing he couldn't honestly tell her. But he would have given everything he owned to be able to do so.

"Allie, I can't tell you your mother is going to be okay, but I can tell you that I'm hoping and praying she is. And that I'm here beside you no matter what."

They stared at each other and then she nodded and laid her head back on his chest. He rested his chin on her head and held her tightly. And prayed she didn't lose someone else she loved.

"I feel helpless and I am so tired of feeling helpless. I know you can't promise me my mother will live but knowing…knowing I could confide in you helps. I'm sorry, I know we're not being personal any more—"

"Not true." He broke into her words. His heart hurt, hurt like a freight train had just smashed through it and blown a tunnel straight through it. Unable to stop himself—not wanting to stop himself, not thinking, not wanting to think, not wanting anything but to comfort her and assure her that they were so far past not getting personal that there was no going back—he dropped his head and kissed her as tenderly as she deserved to be kissed. He longed for more, for the kisses they'd shared before they'd gotten back on track with the all-business deal stated in their contract.

Her sweet lips trembled and he felt her relax against him. Her fingers clenched his shirt against his chest then relaxed and slowly smoothed over his shoulders and around his neck. She sighed softly and it took every bit of concentration to keep the kiss tender. This was about comfort, not passion. She needed a release of the turmoil she was feeling and he'd needed to let her know she was not alone.

Even still, when he forced himself to pull back, his breath was shallow and his heart was on a rampage. "Let's get our things and head to Kerrville."

"Okay. I'll feel better doing that."

"And I'll feel better being by your side."

She looked at him and then nodded, and they went to gather up their things.

CHAPTER EIGHTEEN

There was a Hilton down the road from the rehab center. It was a competitor of the McCoy hotel conglomerate but it was the closest to her mother. He called and had a room booked before they were in the truck. There was a wedding going on and they only had one room left so he took it. They were, after all, married.

As he drove, his hands tightened on the steering wheel. His thoughts were on her mother but more on the fact that if something happened to her, that would mean that Allie would be all alone. She'd have Ginny but no one else. And the truth hit him. It wouldn't matter if she had a whole host of family—he would want to be there for her.

But they couldn't talk about that right now. And they needed something to talk about. "How is your hunt for a shop going for your new florist business?"

Out of the corner of her mouth, he saw her take a deep breath, as if drawing her wits about her. "Good. I think I'm going to relocate it to College Station. It's a busy, growing town and though there is a lot of competition, I feel confident I can carve out a niche for me."

College Station was about halfway between Tyler and Stonewall. Three hours in a truck and a mere hiccup in a plane or helicopter. "That's great."

"Yes, I think it is. I wanted a new start and I love this area. But…well, that's closer than Tyler so if I wanted to take a day trip to Fredericksburg or something…it wouldn't be that far. Or if Ginny wanted to come spend the weekend at my place, then it wouldn't be too far for her. She doesn't realize it but it's good for her to get away from the vineyard some.

She's totally and completely wrapped up in it. I fear she'll never have anything but the vineyard if she keeps up the way she's going. I…I've learned this last little while that I want a balanced life. She needs one, too. I'm going to grow my business but not at the expense of not having a life."

He thought she sounded so in control. So not off-balanced as she'd sounded much of the time when they'd first started this three-month fiasco. "You sound more like a woman with her head on straight."

She turned in the seat and reached her hand out to touch his forearm as he steered the truck. "I'm stronger, Wade. I was shaken by the news of my mother and worried and still am, but on everything else I'm better. I'm probably still a little vulnerable on some things but not on men. I'll never be taken advantage of again. I've learned what to look for in a truly good man and I don't plan to settle for anything less. You helped me know that."

He didn't want her with anyone else.

"I'm honored that you would say that about me." *What was he supposed to say?*

She gently squeezed his arm then drew her hand back. "I'm only stating the truth. I've never met as good a man as you. I'll never forget you."

He closed his eyes momentarily then stared straight ahead, concentrating on getting her to her mother safely.

Her mother was, as she always was, lying so quietly on the bed when they walked into the room. The nurses said that if she didn't improve, they'd be taking her by ambulance the next morning to the hospital to treat her lungs. Bed patients were so susceptible to succumbing to pneumonia that they didn't want to wait around.

Wade went in with her, said a gentle hello to her mom, and then he gave her a hug and told her he'd wait right outside the door for her. If she needed him, she was just to call and he'd be there.

Allie gently took her hand in hers. "Mama, can you hear me? I need you to fight. I need you to come back to me. To open your eyes and sit up in this bed and start moving around. I'm worried you're going to leave me." Allie laid her head on their hands and fought off the tears. Now was not the time for that. "I'm not ready for you to leave me." Her throat ached. "But...I need you to know, that if you need to leave me, I'll be okay." She wished, oh how much she wished she would feel some life in the hand she held. But there was nothing there so she squeezed it just a bit.

"I love you, Mama. I wish you would wake up and meet Wade. You would like him. Remember all the times you told me what kind of man I should grow up and marry? Well, it wasn't conventional, but I married him. And he is as wonderful as you told me he would be. I...just don't get to keep him." She hadn't meant to say the last part but it had come out and with feeling in the words. Allie remembered so clearly the times her mother would talk to her about finding a man who would respect her, and treat her well, and a man who would protect her and stand by her at all cost. She closed her eyes and Wade's image filled the space. Gorgeous, amazing Wade. She really wished her mother could meet him.

She really wished she could keep him.

Wade stood outside the door of Mrs. Jordan's rehab room. The door was cracked open and Allie's words carried through to him. He closed his eyes and let them spring to life inside his heart. *Did she want to keep him?*

Could she really want him like he wanted her?

His mind started to churn. Wade picked up his phone and made a call.

When they left the rehab center and headed to the hotel, Allie was quiet.

"They only had one room," Wade said. "But I figure we can make it work. We're adults, after all. And it's a big bed. I didn't want you to be alone anyway."

"It's fine. We are adults and I really don't want to be alone." She wanted so much more but wouldn't dare say the words. This wasn't that kind of marriage.

There was so much she wanted but she'd signed a contract that she planned to uphold. She had given her word and she didn't plan to complicate Wade's life any more with her wants and needs. She loved him too much for that.

If after the divorce was done and he had his ranch…if he wanted to see her—maybe…hopefully— then maybe she would get the opportunity to tell him how she felt. But if he didn't want to see her anymore, then she saw no need in telling him she had fallen in love with him and making him feel bad because she hadn't listened to his warnings that he would walk away in three months.

No, she told her mother but that was the only person she would ever tell. She didn't even plan to tell Ginny. This was too personal for anyone else to know.

When they walked in the door of the hotel, Wade checked them in. It was obvious the receptionist knew who Wade was and she handed him a large business envelope.

"This came for you, sir."

"Thank you," he said, a look of relief on his face.

He turned back to her and, placing his hand at the base of her spine, he let her go ahead of him. Allie wondered what was in the envelope. When they reached the top floor, they were in a large suite with a king-size bed and a couch with a pullout that Wade quickly pointed out he could use. She didn't want him to use it but she didn't say so.

Wade laid the big tan envelope on the long desk that protruded from the wall, breaking the large room into two sections. "Allie, I wanted to talk to you and I didn't want to do it here in this hotel room but this is something that needs to be talked about in private and I don't want to wait."

Allie didn't know what was going on. He had such an earnest look on his face. "This is fine. What's wrong? You're worrying me."

He gave her a reassuring smile. "I don't want to worry you. But, come here."

She took two steps to him and he took her hands and led her to the blue couch. They sat down, angled toward each other with their knees touching and he continued to hold her hands.

"Allie, I have been torn up these last few weeks. You see, I have a problem. I needed a woman, any woman, to sign a business contract with me and marry me. It seemed so cut-and-dried: she'd get what she wanted and I'd get what I wanted—my dream and the most important thing in the world to me—at the end of three months. At which time the contract would end with a divorce and both our freedoms."

She inhaled, fighting emotions at how non-personal it all seemed.

"Complicated but simple also—if no emotions got involved. And I never dreamed I'd have emotions to deal with. But, Allie, it didn't take long at all for me to have feelings. You came into this with your good, beautiful heart and showed me that everything I believed about women was wrong. That there are good ones out there—I'd just had the misfortune of not finding them. They don't matter, anyway. The fact that you were in my life does. The only problem is I gave my word in that contract. I gave my word that this was strictly business and that is what I felt like you needed too. You had so much on your plate. Ginny reminded me that I didn't need to take advantage of your vulnerable state—"

"I'm not vulnerable anymore."

He placed a finger on her lips. "Shh, I know. I heard you tonight with your mom. I didn't mean to hear, but I did, and I heard the strength of your words. And I also heard them when you talked about your plans for the future. You are a strong woman who has found her way, I believe. But, for me, there is still that darned contract. I had thought that I could wait until the contract ended and then I would come for you. But tonight I realized the truth. Allie, there are divorce papers and a new contract in that envelope that honors your end of the deal. Your mother continues to get the care she needs and you keep the money you are supposed to get. But other than that, we'll be divorced."

"But I don't understand." She couldn't believe what he was saying. "If we divorce, you lose your ranch. You lose everything you ever wanted."

He smiled. "No. I lose the ranch and the oil shares."

"But, still, that's what you love most. And also your brothers lose it too. I can't divorce you yet. We've come so far."

He went down on one knee and she was completely lost. "What?"

"Allie, my brothers will be fine. They don't need the ranch anyway. It's mine to lose or to keep and I have something much, much more important to hopefully bring into my life. You taught me almost from the moment that I met you that people matter. You quickly took over my heart and I realized tonight that I can't wait until the end of the contract. The ranch isn't the most important thing to me—it's you. And you need to know that. I don't care about the ranch. I want you and only you. I'll stand by you now and forever if you'll have me. I love you, Allie, and I want you in my life, as my real wife and not with some crazy contract in our way." He paused and reached for the contract and held it out to her. "It's all there. If you don't feel the way I do, sign it and there is no more obligation for you. You don't need to go through any more days with stress and obligation hanging over you.

I'm here for you no matter what, but I hope you'll marry me for real. We can start a new ranch anywhere. I'm not broke. I can't help who I am but you are more important to me than the ranch."

Allie closed her eyes. *He wanted her. More than he wanted his ranch.* Tears pricked her eyes. She opened them to see his unwavering gaze. She took his face into her hands. "Wade. This doesn't make sense. I love you." She said the words then laughed with relief at finally getting to say the words. "I love you. And no, you can't change who you are. And you can't change the rules about the marriage either. Because, for one, I'm not divorcing you. Ever. And this ranch is going to be yours forever if I have anything to do with it. But also, because when I said those vows, and you kissed me that day, I gave you my heart. Almost from the very start. And I'm not taking it back. You're stuck with me."

The look in his eyes brought her to tears.

"Thank God. I can't lose you, Allie. You mean so much to me. Nothing, and no one, has ever mattered to me as much as you do. When I heard you with your mom, worrying about losing her but willing to let her go if she was ready to go, it killed me. I am not willing to let you go. Not now—not ever. Though I know when our time is up, it's up and we don't really get a say in that. But I do get a say in right now. And right now, I want to spend every day with your smiling face next to mine in the mornings. And with you in my life every day that we are blessed with. I want to show you every day how much I love you and how much you have changed my life."

She was speechless. But it turned out she didn't need to say anything because he pulled her into his arms like a cherished prize and he kissed her, long and slow and well.

And all the weeks of worry, of insecurities about them melted away. *He was hers. Really hers.* As convoluted and crazy as his attempt at trying to give up his ranch for her was, he'd proved to her that she was the most important thing to him. That he needed her as much as she needed him.

She sighed against his lips and gave in to his love. Willingly, totally, completely.

EPILOGUE

"Mama, look at you," Allie said, four weeks later as she walked into her mother's room at the rehab center. Clair Jordan had pulled through that night that Wade had declared his love for Allie and then, a week later, she had come out of the coma and started to improve. It was miraculous and marvelous. And Allie was thankful every day for more time with her mother. Time, she had realized, was precious. So very precious.

"Look at you," Clair said back. "You are beaming, sweet girl."

Her mother was still having a few issues. It would take a little while for her strength to come back and she was able to walk on her own. But she was expected to make a full recovery.

"I'm taking you home today. Are you ready?" All of her rehab could now be done with a specialist coming to the ranch and Allie was so excited to get her mother settled into the home that would be hers as long as she wanted. Wade had made it clear that his home was hers or when she was well, there were other options for her—whatever she wanted. Allie knew her mom, and knew that she was independent and would want her own place as soon as she was able. And that was fine, as long as she was happy. And hopefully near. But for now, she was coming home to the ranch.

Wade came in the door, smiling, and gave Clair a kiss. "Ready to go? Because we're ready to get you out there into the fresh air and sunshine. Might even put you on Ladybug at some point if you want."

"Ladybug? Is that the horse Allie told me about? The gentle one," Clair asked, knowing full well it might be a little while before she could get on a horse.

"That's her, and she's ready to take care of you and show you the ranch from the saddle perspective."

"I always did want to learn to ride but never had the opportunity."

Allie's heart was full as Wade pushed her mother's wheelchair from the room. It just seemed too good to be true.

He smiled at her over his shoulder. "You coming?"

She nodded and smiled so big her face hurt as he winked then took up the conversation with her mother, telling her how Ladybug was the perfect horse for her to learn on and that they'd have her in the saddle before long.

Allie walked behind them, so happy she could explode. The contract had ended that morning, and Wade and she both were free to do as they pleased and they pleased to be together forever.

She had had all kinds of disasters hit her life that had put her working in that truck stop that fateful night that Wade had walked in and told her those crazy terms of the will.

As they walked out into the sunshine, she felt that sense of wonder...and gratitude that she had been there that night when he'd walked in and changed her life.

As he got her mother settled in the backseat of the truck and then placed the wheelchair in the bed of the truck, she placed her arms around his waist and kissed him.

He smiled against her lips. "What's that for?"

"For being you. I love you, Wade."

He looked into her eyes and she saw her future there.

"Darlin', I love you too. And I'm so glad today is here and we are free from all that craziness."

"Craziness that brought us together. Because if it hadn't been for your granddaddy, we wouldn't have found each other."

"True. I'm forever grateful to him. And I know he's smiling."

"I think so too. When does the next domino fall?"

He grimaced. "We have to be at Mr. Emerson's tomorrow. And we'll see what the next step is."

"Who do you think it will be? Todd or Morgan?"

He laughed. "I'm not sure but I can tell you that neither one of them is going to be happy."

She smiled. "It should be interesting to watch. I kind of like the way Granddaddy thinks."

Wade grinned and kissed her. "I do too. But they don't, so the fireworks will be something fierce, I think. But I don't care—I've got my prize and wouldn't change anything."

She wouldn't either.

Check out the next book in the McCoy Billionaire Brothers series, HER BILLIONAIRE COWBOY'S WEDDING FIASCO

About the Author

Hope Moore is the pen name of an award-winning author who lives deep in the heart of Texas surrounded by Christian cowboys who give her inspiration for all of her inspirational sweet romances. She loves writing clean & wholesome, swoon worthy romances for all of her fans to enjoy and share with everyone. Her heartwarming, feel good romances are full of humor and heart, and gorgeous cowboys and heroes to love. And the spunky women they fall in love with and live happily-ever-after.

When she isn't writing, she's trying very hard not to cook, since she could live on peanut butter sandwiches, shredded wheat, coffee...and cheesecake why should she cook? She loves writing though and creating new stories is her passion. Though she does love shoes, she's admitted she has an addiction and tries really hard to stay out of shoe stores. She, however, is not addicted to social media and chooses to write instead of surf FB - but she LOVES her readers so she's working on a free novella just for you and if you sign up for her newsletter she will send it to you as soon as its ready! You'll also receive snippets of her adventures, along with special deals, sneak peaks of soon-to-be released books and of course any sales she might be having.

She promises she will not spam you, she hates to be spammed also, so she wouldn't dare do that to people she's crazy about (that means YOU). You can unsubscribe at any time.

Sign up for my newsletter:
www.subscribepage.com/hopemooresignup

I can't wait to hear from you.

Hope Moore~
Always hoping for more love, laughter and reading for you every day of your life!